Courage and Dust

Sanderson Ridge Book 2

Includes bonus prequel

All Wrapped Up

Alicia Hitchcock

All Wrapped Up

A Sanderson Ridge Christmas

Alicia Hitchcock

ISBN: 978-0-6483578-9-6

Chapter 1
Kit

December 22

Kit yawned and stretched her arms up, twisting her body from side to side as she got out of bed. It was going to be a long day, and a hot one by the feel of it. She glanced at her watch. 7 am and the sun was already well above the horizon. She looked down at Will. His face, unguarded and peaceful, had a boyish quality that melted her heart and brought a smile to her face. But they didn't have time to linger. She lay back down on the bed and leaned close to his ear.

'Rise and shine, spunky bum,' she whispered. He groaned and opened one eye.

'It's not time to get up yet. Is it?' Kit laughed, then rolled off the bed and headed for the bathroom. By the time she returned, dressed in denim shorts and a black shirt, with her brunette hair tied in a messy bun, Will was slipping into his boots.

The football oval and grounds around it were already buzzing with activity by the time they arrived. Will and Kit's dad, Tom, went to set up the dunking tank, which was a fundraiser for the organising committee. Kit looked around. The football oval had been neatly mown in preparation for the day's festivities. It was surrounded by bushy shrubs on one side, a brick building that housed the club rooms on the other, and two sets of stands. The scoreboard on the far side of the oval still announced the Sanderson Ridge Raiders' premiership win over the Merredin Football Club from months earlier.

Walking towards the row of gazebos that were being set up, Kit spotted Mrs Higgins at the Community Resource Centre's activity stall. Sandra Ferguson was setting up her sewing and knitting on a table, and Paula Jackson was working on her display of handmade jewellery. Beth burst through between two parked cars, almost knocking Kit over.

'Sorry. I didn't see you there,' Beth said. That wasn't surprising considering she was laden with three trays full of baked goods. Lara was right behind her with two more trays.

'No worries. Do you need a hand?' Kit asked.

'That'd be great. There's more in the back of my van.' Kit grabbed two trays and made her way back through to the stalls.

'It feels like it's going to be a hot one,' Lara said, looking up at the sun already high in the sky.

'Yeah. The weather's unpredictable. I remember when I was growing up, there were years when these Christmas fairs were rained out,' Kit said. Kit had lived her entire life in Sanderson Ridge. Nestled in the middle of Western Australia, it was a town that had been bucking the trend and growing instead of shrinking in population. The mountain range that was the backbone of the town was a drawcard for tourists, and some of them stayed, boosting the population to just over 1200. The old sandstone pub had been in operation since 1905; the council chambers were newly built; and Beth had turned a house on the main street into a thriving café. The small school had three classrooms, and next to it stood a nature playground and a skate park. It was still a small country town, but it was far more vibrant than it had been when Kit was younger.

'There you are,' a familiar voice said. Kit pivoted to find her best friend Angela standing with her hands on her hips.

'It's not her fault, Ang. I commandeered her to help with this lot,' Beth said, arranging cupcakes in neat rows.

'All good,' Angela said, then turned to Kit. 'Charlotte needs a hand.' Kit and Angela walked across the oval to the stage where Angela's sister was giving orders. The constant hum of voices, mixed with the sounds of hammering and engines turning over, filled the air. More people were arriving, setting up stalls and rides, or positioning machinery and herding animals into pens for display. The Sanderson Ridge Christmas Fair had started when the town was founded in 1905. It had grown from a few stalls to a vibrant fete that drew enormous crowds from the surrounding districts. This year looked to be no exception.

Kit spotted Will helping Angela's boyfriend and neighbour, Nate, hoist the advertising banners for the Shire and the co-op that was sponsoring the fair. The banners fluttered in the light breeze. Kit flicked the hair out of her face and waved as Will looked up. He beamed, and Kit's heart thumped a little quicker. She'd been with Will for two years now. He was kind, funny, hardworking, and ruggedly handsome in that way that men who work with their hands seem to be. He'd been travelling, getting work on stations for a few months, before moving on to the next town. But when he'd landed in Sanderson Ridge to work on the McGregor farm, he'd bumped into Kit at the pub one night. The rest was history. Now, they lived in a poky two-bedroom house on the edge of the cattle farm that had been in her family for generations. Will worked the farm with her dad, and when Kit wasn't helping them, she did a few shifts a week at the pub.

The sound of a loud crash startled Kit, who turned to see some guys from the football team picking up a fallen metal pole as they built the stage. Near the main entrance gate, the stage was the centrepiece of the fair. It was where the shire president and CEO would give speeches, where the local schoolkids would perform Christmas carols, and where Kit would be giving a concert. If she could call it that. It was six songs. And they weren't even her own; it was public karaoke.

'Hey, can you grab that box for me?' Charlotte called out to Angela, then turned to Kit. 'What do you think?'

'Gorgeous, as always. Very festive,' Kit said, admiring the decorations Charlotte had already hung up on the supporting poles and laid out along the front of the stage. Kit grabbed a bunched-up string of lights and started unravelling the tangled mess.

'I love Christmas, don't you? There's something about it that brings people together. It's got new beginnings and second chances vibes,' Charlotte said, waving around a glitter-covered star before placing it on top of the tree she'd erected on the side of the stage.

Angela snorted. 'I don't know about all that, but it is a good time of year for winding down and relaxing, especially after the year we've had,' she said. Charlotte shrugged a shoulder and continued with her task. Kit was more inclined to agree with Angela than Charlotte. Stretching to attach the unravelled lights along the front of the stage, Kit toppled forward and landed with her hands in the dirt. Silently cursing her clumsiness, she looked up as she stood and wiped her hands on her jeans. Will and Angela were huddled on the other side of the stage, hands gesticulating wildly. They fell silent as she approached.

'I've got to help Nate. See you later on. Keep an eye out for us in the tractor parade,' Angela said, before making her way over to the group of men gathered around the machinery. Kit turned her attention to Will, eyes narrowed.

'What were you two whispering about?' Kit asked.

'Nothing. Ang is worried you might be getting nervous, that's all,' Will said. She wasn't performing until the evening, but there was already a gnawing feeling in Kit's stomach. Obviously, she wasn't hiding it as well as she thought. Singing in public like this was poles apart from bashing out a couple of songs in the pub.

'You're going to rock it,' Charlotte said, breezing past them with tinsel trailing in her wake.

'Thanks. It's just a few songs. It'll be fine,' Kit said, picking up the lights again.

'Charlotte's right. You'll be great. I reckon it's going to be a special night,' Will said, a grin spread across his face. Kit wasn't sure about that. It seemed as though Charlotte's infectiously optimistic attitude had rubbed off on Will.

Chapter 2
Tom

Tom stood and stretched his arms up and back. He was strong for a man in his early 60s; he had to be, but the aches and pains still crept in from time to time. He lifted his hat, wiped his brow, then shoved his hat back on and got back to work. Shirley and Beth had asked him to help set up the gazebos and trestle tables for the stallholders, who were already arriving and unpacking their goods. Beth approached with a carrot cupcake and a coffee.

'Here. Payment for your help,' she said, handing it to him.

'Thanks. You didn't have to.'

'I've got plenty more where that came from.' Beth looked around the oval. 'Things are starting to feel very festive. I love this time of year. How about you?' Tom took a sip of coffee before answering.

'It used to be a highlight, but ever since Kate died, it's just never been the same. Everyone's off with their families. And now Kit has Will...' he trailed off, unsure of how much he wanted to divulge about his feelings. Charlotte eyed him for a second, her gaze lingering.

'I've been thinking about approaching Shirley about having a Christmas lunch at the pub for those of us who don't have family close by, or who just want a bit of company for a while.'

'Sounds like a good idea. I reckon a few people around here would be interested.'

'That settles it then,' Beth said. She gave him the thumbs up and then headed towards the far end of the row of stalls, where Shirley was talking with a red-headed woman who had her back turned to him. Tom finished his cupcake and downed the rest of his coffee, then set up the last gazebo and headed for the group of men standing near the machinery.

Nate, Kane, and Will were huddled around a new yellow and green tractor. The price on the sales sheet in the window put it way out of their grasp, but that didn't stop them from checking it out. Tom folded his arms and leaned against the side of the engine bay, catching the last of their conversation.

'Be good for the co-op,' Nate said. The others agreed. Tom felt eyes on him and looked up into Will's face. The younger man jerked his head to the side and then walked off. Tom frowned, then followed. Was there a problem with the co-op? Will stood away from the others and put his hands in his pockets, then took them out and wrung them, before putting them back in again.

'Is everything alright? You look pale,' Tom said.

'Yeah. It's just...I...um. Tom, this is a bit formal, but I feel like it's the right thing to do.' Tom's gut clenched. He had an inkling of where this conversation was headed.

'Out with it then.' He folded his arms but found it hard to hide the smirk on his face. He'd let Will suffer for a bit first.

'I'd like to ask you for Kit's hand in marriage,' Will blurted. Tom tried to hold his stance, but a moment later his face broke into a grin and he slapped Will on the back.

'As if I have a say in it. You know Kit. But in any case, you have my blessing.' Tom could practically see the relief wash over Will. He thought back to the day he'd done the same thing with Kate's dad. He was nervous as hell, and Kate's dad was formidable, but he'd managed to get the words out. He and Kate were married for thirty wonderful years. 'You look like you could use a drink. I think the bar's open in the clubrooms.'

'Bit early, isn't it? It's only 11.' Tom waved off his comment and they fell into step, headed to the clubrooms on the other side of the oval.

✪

Will was stopped by Shane McGregor, so Tom told him he'd meet him at the bar. He opened the door to the clubrooms and was about to walk in when the red-headed woman he'd seen earlier walked out with her face buried in her phone.

'Sorry,' she said, then lifted her head. Tom's jaw dropped, his expression mirrored on the woman's face. It wasn't her. It couldn't be. He closed his eyes and shook his head slightly, then opened them again. She was still standing in front of him, but her expression had shifted from surprise to something akin to annoyance.

'Tom Brady, as I live and breathe.'

'Cynthia Douglas. Here for the fair, are you?' The woman pursed her lips. She was still as beautiful as she had been when they were seventeen, although time had added a few lines around her eyes and on her forehead. Tom's eyes flicked to his reflection in the door. He hadn't fared quite as well.

'Not that it's any of your business, but I have a stall. And I'd best be getting back to it.'

'Rightio,' Tom nodded. He wanted to say something that would keep the conversation going, but his mind was blank. There was too much water under that bridge anyway. He moved aside to let her pass and watched her walk into the crowd, his body betraying his true feelings.

'Who was that?' Kit's voice called out when he got inside. He groaned inwardly. That girl never missed a thing. He was surprised she had no idea what Will was planning. Or perhaps she did and was hiding it. She had a tendency to wear masks in public.

'Nobody,' he said. Kit glared at him, and he rolled his eyes. 'Her name is Cynthia Douglas. Or at least it was when we were in high school.' Tom could almost see the cogs rotating in Kit's head. He turned to the barman to avoid her scrutiny and ordered a beer. The less he said about his dealings with Cynthia Douglas, the better.

Chapter 3
Kit

The roar of twenty tractor engines and the giggles of excited children filled the air. The Christmas-themed banners on the poles dotted in the median strip fluttered in the breeze. People were crowded along both sides of the main street of Sanderson Ridge. Kids were dressed in festive outfits complete with Santa hats or sparkly headbands. Anticipation hung heavy in the air. Kit stood on the footpath outside the Imperial Hotel with Charlotte, Beth, and Shirley.

'Here they come,' someone shouted nearby, and all heads turned to watch the tractor parade make its way down the main street and out towards the football field and Christmas fair. Laurence Hopkins, the shire CEO, dressed in a Santa outfit complete with phony white hair and beard, drove the lead tractor. The shire staff had decorated it to look like Santa's sleigh, and as it slowly ambled past, some staff and councillors who were sitting in the attached trailer threw lollies to the children in the crowd. The kids dived and jumped to catch as many as their little hands could hold. Next in line was Richard Kellerman in a brand new tractor adorned with reindeer cutouts. Kit felt Charlotte stiffen next to her. Richard had made her and Angela's lives harder after their parents had passed away. Even though they'd sorted out their differences, there was still some lingering animosity between them. Nate's old red tractor was next. He and Angela, who was riding in the trailer with their dogs, Josie, Pippa, and Bizkit, had created Santa's workshop. Angela tried to wrangle the dogs, their elf ears flapping as they sat up and looked around at the crowd. Tom and Will passed the group. Their tractor, thanks to Kit's decorating skills, had about 100 metres of red, green, and silver tinsel wrapped around every protruding part.

'It's definitely been Kitified,' Charlotte said, nudging Kit.

'What can I say? I love sparkly stuff,' Kit said, grinning. The other women burst into laughter.

Kit, Beth, Charlotte, and Shirley watched the rest of the parade, clapping along as each tractor drove past. The crowd began to disperse, most heading for the fair.

'What a ripper.' Shirley said, then nodded her head towards the pub. 'I'd better open up or there'll be an outcry. See you later on.' Shirley turned and headed inside.

'That was a fantastic parade. Everyone put in so much effort. I'd better get back to the fair and help Lara out, though,' Beth said. 'She gets a bit overwhelmed when there are too many customers at once.'

'We'll come with you,' Kit said, linking arms with Charlotte.

The fair was in full swing by the time they arrived back. People were scattered all over the oval, around the grounds, and inside the clubrooms. Music blared from speakers, children and teens screamed from the rides, women perused the craft and cake stalls, and men crowded around machinery and farm animals. Kit and Charlotte went in search of Angela and found her and Will standing next to Tom's tractor. Kit sidled up and pecked Will on the lips. He pulled her in tight for a quick hug.

'What did you think?' he asked them.

'I reckon this one looked blindingly good,' Charlotte said, pointing to the tractor. Kit glanced at Angela. She'd been quieter than usual that morning. There was something on her mind. Kit grabbed her by the hand.

'Come on. You look like you could use a bit of fun,' she said, pulling her toward the rides. They made their way through the throng and stood in front of a stomach-churning ride. Kit bought tickets and they waited in line.

'Are you going to tell me what's up with you today?' Kit asked. Angela shifted from one foot to the other, scrutinising the ride's movement.

'There's nothing wrong. I just didn't sleep well, and it's going to be a long day, that's all.' Angela folded her arms and kept her gaze away from Kit's. She wasn't ready to talk and Kit knew not to press her. They took their seats on the ride and both screamed as they were whisked high into the air and back down at an alarming speed. The adrenaline put a smile on Angela's face, and she was in better spirits as they made their way back over to the stalls. Kit waved at her dad as they walked past the dunk tank.

Kit and Angela slowly made their way up one side of the alley that the stalls formed. Kit's eyes were drawn to the jewellery stand, and she bought a pair of turquoise and silver earrings. She stopped at the next stall and rummaged through a rack of colourful flowing skirts. Pulling one out, she held it up against her body. Looking up again, she spotted her dad and the redheaded woman he'd been speaking with earlier. They passed by one another, trying to avoid each other's gaze. Clearly, there was more to the story than her dad was letting on.

'You want that skirt, Kit?' a man asked. 'You could wear it tonight.' Kit glanced over and saw fellow karaoke contestant, Gazza. He and Kit had been competing against each other for the last few years. His angelic voice didn't match the gruff exterior, and he always got the crowd pumped up. He'd been gracious in defeat when she'd won the competition earlier in the year.

'I'll get it. Thanks. I've got my outfit already planned for tonight, though.' She handed the skirt to Gazza, and he put it in a bag and passed her the machine to swipe her card.

'You all set then?'

'Yeah. It's not much different from the pub,' Kit said. Gazza's mouth twisted to one side.

'I don't know about that. There's a heck of a lot more people here than at the Imperial on a Saturday night. I don't think I could do what you're about to do. But more power to you. You'll nail it.' Kit swallowed and took the proffered bag. Was everyone trying to make her nervous? She wanted to do the concert; she'd practised for weeks. But now that the day was here, it was a different story. She said goodbye and went to look for Angela, putting the concert out of her mind. That was a problem for later. For now, she just wanted to enjoy the festivities.

Chapter 4
Tom

Sweat beaded on Tom's brow as he plunged his hand into the cool dunk tank water, splashing his face to relieve the sweltering afternoon heat. Signalling for Shane to take over, he worked his way through the crowd towards the clubrooms. A young family with a pram stopped in front of him. He wove his way around them, only to find himself face to face with Cynthia. He went left and so did she; then they both tried to go right. Cynthia put her hands up in surrender, a look of frustration on her face.

'I'll go left,' she said. Tom nodded and passed on her right. The scent of lavender and jasmine perfume filled his nostrils. The smell transported him straight back to his teen years, making his groin twitch. He turned back to look at her.

'Cynthia...' he called out. She turned and shook her head, then walked away. Tom's shoulders fell, and his stomach churned. He knew he'd hurt her, but hadn't the years softened the blow? He let out a long sigh and made his way inside.

Grabbing a soft drink from the bar, he spotted Will, who was nursing a beer in the far corner of the room. Tom sat across from him and took in the 'deer in the headlights' look in Will's eyes.

'You alright?' Tom asked. Will shook his head, then nodded, and finally shrugged. Tom let out a low laugh. 'You'll be fine, mate. It's pretty clear to anyone who's seen you two together that Kit loves you. She'll say yes.'

'But what if I stuff up the proposal somehow?' Will said, then took a swig of beer. Tom's brows knitted together.

'You'll be fine. Just don't have too many of those.' Will looked at his glass as if noticing it for the first time.

'Right. Yeah. That's it. No more for me. I've got to be on my game.'

'I reckon you're making this out to be bigger than it needs to be.'

'I just want it to go right. For Kit,' Will said. Kit had found a good lad. He wondered if Kate's dad had thought the same of him all those years ago. Lost in thought, Tom jolted when Angela sat at the table.

'How's the station stay going?' he asked her.

'It's going really well. We're practically booked solid for the next year. Thanks to some influencers getting behind it.'

'And your marketing skills, no doubt,' Tom said. Angela thanked him, then turned her attention to Will.

'All set?' she asked. Tom looked between the two of them. Will swallowed, then bit his bottom lip.

'It's okay. Ang knows,' he said to Tom, then looked at Angela. 'I reckon I've got it sorted.'

'Care to share the details?' Tom asked, feeling out of the loop. They both shook their heads.

'The less people who know, the better,' Angela said. Tom raised a hand.

'Right. Well, I might go and see if Nate needs a hand at the co-op stand.' He waved at the two of them. They seemed to have it all in hand. It sounded like the big question was going to be popped soon. Perhaps after the concert tonight. Kit would see it as a sign, especially if her performance was a hit.

✪

The next few hours passed quickly. Tom had spent the afternoon helping at a few different stalls. Nate's co-op information stall had been popular, and he'd helped sign up two new farmers who'd recently moved to the district. Now, he sat at the bottom of the grandstand watching the people below him move around like busy ants. He looked at his watch. He should probably head home and freshen up before the concert. He stood and stretched, then spotted movement out of the corner of his eye. Cynthia walked towards him, and he had the chance to assess her appearance again. She still had a svelte figure, and the dark green dress she was wearing accentuated her curves and made her almost ruby red hair brighter. Tom smoothed down his clothes, conscious that he'd been sweating in them all day.

'Can we sit? Have a chat?' she asked. He nodded. They sat with a hand span of space between them. Tom wanted to look at her, but kept his eyes on the fair. He waited, his stomach in knots. After a full minute, he turned and saw that she was scrutinising him.

'You still look the same,' she said.

'So do you.'

'The fair looks like a success,' she said, turning back to the crowd. The small talk was killing Tom, but he didn't want to force them into what he knew would be an argument. Things between them needed to go slowly. Lest someone get hurt again.

'I heard about Kate. I'm sorry.' Tom thanked her and waited. Her fidgeting told him she had something on her mind. 'I just thought I should let you know that I'm thinking of moving back to the Ridge.' Tom's mouth opened and closed. He didn't know what he'd been expecting, but it wasn't that. He recovered from the shock.

'That's great. The town's changed a bit since we were younger, but I'm sure you'll love it. It's still got that small-town feel.' Cynthia nodded, then slapped her hands on her thighs and stood up.

'Right. That's that.' She turned to go, and Tom stood up.

'Cynthia, wait. We should talk.'

'There's nothing to talk about. I guess I'll see you round.' She walked down the stands and disappeared into the crowd, leaving Tom reeling. If that was the way she wanted to play this, then he'd go with it. But at some point, he should tell her the truth. He had to.

Chapter 5
Kit

Crowds were thick inside the fair, and people were still coming through the gates. Kit had spent the afternoon helping Beth and Lara with their stall. Bath's reputation as an amazing cook had got around, and they were run off their feet. Kit had just finished a short sound check and was ready to head home and get ready for the concert. She wove her way through the crowds and into the parking area. Tom and Will stood near the car, speaking in hushed tones. Kit walked between two parked cars, keeping an eye on the two men. If she could just get close enough, she might find out what was going on. Crouched down pretending to fix the strap on her sandal, Kit strained to hear, but their voices were too low. Two clean brown boots moved into her line of vision, and she rose to look into Laurence Hopkins' smiling face.

'Not long until the show,' he said. 'We're all looking forward to it.' Kit straightened her spine.

'Yeah? That's great. I can't wait to get up there,' she said, with a smile plastered on her face. Laurence looked across the bonnet of the car and spotted Will and Tom. He walked over, and Kit followed.

'G'Day Tom. I saw Cynthia Douglas earlier. She tells me she's moving back. Bit of a blast from the past, hey?' Laurence said, gently punching Tom on the shoulder. Tom grimaced, and his eyes flew to Kit, his face pale. She glanced from one man to the other, her stomach tightening into a knot.

'What do you mean?' she asked Laurence. She knew her dad hadn't been completely honest with her earlier, and she was determined to find out why. Laurence smirked.

'Cynthia and your dad were an item back in the day. But something happened between them. Next thing we all knew, Cynthia had moved to Geraldton and Tom was moping around.' Kit's eyebrows shot up. Her dad had had another girlfriend. Why had she never heard about this? Had he been two-timing her mum? Kit felt her breath come a little faster, but she tilted her head and forced a smile.

'Really? When was this? What year?' she asked. Recognition dawned on Laurence's face.

'Don't worry. It was before he and your mum got together.' The group fell silent until Will moved towards the driver's door.

'We'd better get going if we want to be back in time for the start of the concert. I know how long you take to get ready,' he said, winking at Kit. Laurence said goodbye, but not before mouthing 'sorry' to Tom. Kit sat in the passenger seat, trying to process her thoughts. Her dad had a girlfriend before he got with her mum. And that woman was back in Sanderson Ridge. It shouldn't be a big deal. It was completely normal for teenagers and young adults to have several relationships. But it still gave her an uneasy feeling. Her dad had loved someone other than her mum. Her parents' marriage was her relationship yardstick. They had laughed and danced and joked around, but they'd also stuck by each other through some incredibly hard times, too. She had always thought she wanted a marriage like that. Now she wondered how much of it was real.

✪

The sun dipped below the horizon, and the fair transformed, bursting into the night with hundreds of twinkling lights. Families were dotted on picnic blankets in front of the stage. Young children danced to modern renditions of Christmas carols. The screams of teenagers on the carnival rides could be heard when the music paused. From her vantage point backstage, Kit spotted Will, Angela, Nate, Kane, and Charlotte standing together close to the other side of the stage. Will's smile looked forced. Was he worried about her performance? Her own concern had morphed from worry into excitement just as she'd hoped.

She looked down at her red empire-line dress and strappy silver high heels. She'd spent so much time on her hair and makeup that they'd nearly been late back to town. She took out her phone and snapped a selfie before posting it on social media. The music died down, and everyone quieted as Laurence took to the stage. He kept his speech short, thanking sponsors and mentioning the shire office closures.

'Now, let's get the party started. Our singer tonight needs no introduction. She's a born and bred Sanderson Ridge girl with an incredible singing voice. Please join me in welcoming the very talented Kit Brody,' he said. The crowd clapped as Kit made her way onto the stage. Butterflies filled her stomach as she thanked Laurence and asked the crowd if they were ready for some fun. The biggest cheers came from her friends. She blew a kiss to Will, then turned around to signal the band. The first few bars of *All I Want for Christmas* started. It was go-time. Any nerves she'd felt dissipated as she sang and shimmied her way around the stage. As the crowd sang along, the kids' laughter echoed through the air as they danced in circles. Kit couldn't wipe the smile off her face as she caught her breath between songs.

Replacing the microphone on the stand, readying herself for the next track, Kit spotted Will standing at the side of the stage. She beamed at him, then stepped up to the microphone and addressed the crowd.

'Are we ready for another song?' Kit called out. The crowd cheered. Kit waited for the beat, and when it didn't come, she turned around to face the band. None of them held their instruments. Why weren't they ready? If they kept this up, the crowd would start to get annoyed. Kit waved her hand, trying to get the attention of the guitarist, but he was focused on something to her right. She turned and saw Will walking towards her. She shook her head slightly. Did he realise he'd walked out onto the stage? He strode towards her and then stumbled forward with his hands in front of him. His left foot was wrapped up in the power cords crisscrossing the stage. He tried to yank it free to no avail. Kit grabbed his arm as he took a tumble.

'What are you doing up here?' She whispered in his ear as she steadied him. His eyes were wide and his face was pale. 'Are you alright? You don't look well.'

'I...This...' he said, floundering, his eyes as big as saucers. The crowd murmured, and a few people coughed. Will looked out towards the crowd, shifting his eyes towards their friends, and then back at Kit.

'Will? What's going on?' Kit asked, covering the microphone with one hand. He looked at her, and his lip trembled.

'I'm sorry,' he mumbled, then bent down and unhooked his foot before running off the stage and out of sight. What the heck was that all about? Kit felt torn. She should go after him and see if he was alright. But the crowd was getting restless. She looked over to where her friends stood. Angela had her head in her hands. But the others looked just as confused as Kit felt. Charlotte raised her hands and mouthed, 'I don't know. ' Why would Will come onto the stage in the middle of her show? Whatever he was going to do, he'd changed his mind and left her looking like a fool in front of hundreds of people. A man's voice broke through Kit's thoughts.

'Keep going. Deal with it later,' Laurence called out from the side of the stage. Kit took a deep breath and let her shoulders relax. The show must go on. She turned back to the band. This time, they had their instruments in hand. The guitarist gave her a thumbs-up, so she stepped up to the microphone again.

'It looks as though someone's been into the eggnog,' she said. Some of the crowd laughed. 'Let's get on with the show,' she yelled. The crowd clapped, and the band started the first chords of *Last Christmas*. Kit busted out the next few songs in her set, shimmying around the stage and working the crowd.

'That's it for us, folks. Merry Christmas!' With a deep bow, she gestured toward the band, and then bowed again. A chorus of clapping, cheering, and whistling erupted from the crowd. Despite the interruption, it seemed that the show had been a success. She waved as she ran off the stage, determined to find Will and figure out what was going on.

Chapter 6
Tom

Tom stood in the crowd and watched Kit leave the stage, his chest tight and shoulders heavy. He knew what Will was trying to do when he'd gone on stage, but nobody else did, especially Kit. She'd looked confused, but she'd soldiered on. She could put on a mask for the rest of the world, but Tom had always been able to see through it. Kit had hidden her embarrassment. Tom made his way through the crowd and caught the end of a few comments.

'...mucked that up.'

'...would have done it better.'

Tom sighed and tried to ignore them. He'd lived in small towns all his life. He knew how fast gossip travelled. Before the night was over, everyone in town would have heard about Will's spectacular failure on stage.

Tom walked on, determined to make sure Kit was alright. He found her and Will standing behind the stage, faces scowling, arms flailing. Stopping near some scaffolding, he watched them for a few moments. Kit's face was scrunched up like she was about to cry. Will didn't look much better. Had Will told her what he'd tried to do? Tom backed away. It was their business. He'd pick up the pieces later if he needed to. He turned to leave and spotted Cynthia packing up the last remnants of her stall. He watched her for a moment. Their conversation earlier had left him frustrated. There were so many things left unsaid. They might as well be said now.

'Need a hand?' he asked as he approached her. She spun around, almost dropping the box she was carrying.

'Oh! No, thanks. I've got it.'

'Are you sure?'

'I can handle things on my own. I learnt that a long time ago. Thanks to you.' Her words struck like a blow to the stomach. Seeing that she'd hit her mark, she turned and stormed off towards the row of cars behind the stalls. Tom ran after her.

'Cynthia, can we talk about it? Please?' She opened the car door and shoved the box into the back seat. When she turned back, the festive lights hung around the stalls showed the anger in her eyes.

'There's nothing to talk about. I thought we loved each other. I thought we were going to have a life together. But instead, you chose to stay in Sanderson Ridge over moving to Geraldton with me.'

'That's not what happened.'

'Save it,' she said, holding her hand up. 'Look, Tom. I don't want to go over this anymore. What's done is done. Let's just leave it.' Tom stood rooted to the spot. The urge to say more gnawed at him, but she clearly didn't want to have that discussion. It would be easier to leave old wounds alone than to tell her the truth. She looked up at him, the light reflecting the tears gleaming in her eyes. He watched her drive away, pain gripping his chest.

✪

The sun was up before Tom's alarm buzzed. He rolled out of bed and stretched, wincing at the pain in his lower back. He'd overdone it yesterday, but he wasn't about to back out when there was work to be done. He dressed and made his way out to the shed. The wind through the driver's window whipped through what was left of his greying hair as he drove his ute towards the paddocks. He pulled a bag of feed off the back and filled the steel trough. The water level was fine today, but it would need a top-up tomorrow. He methodically went through his daily tasks, grateful to be busy enough that his mind stopped thinking about his last encounter with Cynthia. Sleep was elusive, and he'd tossed and turned most of the night. The look on Cynthia's face before she drove away played over in his mind. It was still there as he made his way back inside the house.

Kit was standing at the stove cooking bacon and eggs. The toaster popped, and she turned around, her eyes red-rimmed. Tom grabbed two plates and buttered the toast. The only time Kit slept in her old bedroom rather than the little house a few hundred metres from the homestead was when she'd had an argument with Will. It had only happened twice so far. Once, when Will went on a boys' trip to Perth without telling her beforehand, and another time when she'd lost the karaoke competition and Will hadn't been as supportive as she'd hoped. Both times, they'd made up before the morning was over.

Tom sat at the table as Kit placed the plate in front of him. Cutting off a corner of toast and smearing it with runny egg, he shoved the forkful in his mouth. Kit sipped her coffee, barely touching her food. Tom cleared his throat. Since Kate had died, he'd taken on the role of mother and father, but he still found talking things out uncomfortable, especially when it involved relationship issues.

'Do you want to talk about it?' he asked, shoving the last of his toast into his mouth. Kit shook her head and looked out the back door. Tom sat back and waited. Kit turned to him.

'It was so embarrassing, Dad. He made a fool of himself, and of me, in front of everyone. He wouldn't even tell me what he was doing on the stage.'

Tom took a deep breath. 'It wasn't that bad, love. You got on with it, and everyone enjoyed the concert. I heard quite a few people say how talented you are.'

'Did you also hear them say how we mucked it up?'

'Nah. Not at all.' Tom said. A white lie wouldn't hurt in this situation. He had to soothe his daughter without giving Will's secret away. 'Look, Kit. Will loves you. He stuffed up, but he's a good bloke. I don't think what happened warrants this sort of reaction.' Kit shrugged and downed the last of her coffee.

'Well, he shouldn't be keeping secrets from me. Nobody should.' She shot daggers at him, then stalked to her bedroom and slammed the door. Tom rubbed his face with his hands and groaned. Kit would have to learn that some secrets were meant to be kept.

Chapter 7
Kit

December 23

The house was quiet, but that didn't mean Kit was alone. Her dad was a reserved man. The yin to her mum's outgoing yang. Kit was glad she took after her mother. She crept out of her childhood bedroom towards the kitchen, cursing the creaking floorboard at the end of the hallway. Her dad's car wasn't in the driveway, but she could see Will walking towards the house. She grunted and went to check her appearance in the hallway mirror. She smoothed back her hair into a high ponytail. It was good enough. Will came in the back door and called out to her. She breezed into the dining room and sat down, folding her arms on the table in front of her. Will plonked into the chair across from her. If the dark circles under his eyes were anything to go by, he'd had a rough night too.

'Can we talk about last night?' he asked.

'Sure. If you want to tell me what's really going on,' she said, her eyes boring into him. He shifted in his seat and swallowed.

'It was going to be a surprise.'

'What was?'

'I thought that was going to be the perfect time to do it. Ang didn't agree.'

'What does Angela have to do with this?'

'Nothing. She was just helping me bring it all together.'

Kit let out a frustrated sigh. 'Bring what together. You haven't told me anything.' They both stared at each other for a long moment before Will took a deep breath and let his shoulders droop.

'I was trying to propose.' Kit's jaw dropped. A proposal? In front of the whole district? That was not what she had expected him to say. She hadn't even thought about them getting married. They were good together, just as they were. Why did he want to change things? She pushed back from the table and stood.

'I need to go and help clean up at the footy club.'

Will's brow knitted together. 'I just told you I want to marry you, and you've got nothing to say about it?'

She shook her head. 'I think I need some space.'

'Kit, don't do this.'

'I'm sorry,' she said, turning and walking to her bedroom. She closed the door and put her back against it, sliding down to the floor, tears streaming down her face. Why had she reacted like that? She loved Will, and he clearly loved her. But proposing to her in front of the entire district. That wasn't how she'd wanted an intimate moment like that to play out.

Sure, she was outgoing, but some things were too special to share. Why did the men in her life not know her well enough? Her dad had kept secrets, and so had Will. Will had a good reason to, but even so. It just didn't feel right. The idea of marriage, the proposal. None of it. And Christmas was in two days. What about the Christmas dinner she had planned? Was it even going to go ahead? Everything was such a mess.

✪

The queue for Beth's was almost out the door, but Kit knew the coffee was worth it. Plus, she needed a sweet pick-me-up, and Beth's chocolate croissant was to die for. She stood in line doomscrolling on her phone when she felt a nudge in her side.

'Hey, how did it go last night? Everything sorted out now?' Angela asked, looking at Kit's left hand and frowning. Kit shoved her hands in her pockets.

'No, actually. It's not. Why didn't you tell me what Will was planning?'

'Oh, come on! I couldn't do that. The friend code doesn't extend to this.' She leaned in closer to avoid eavesdroppers. 'A proposal should be a surprise. I know Will mucked it up, but his intentions were good. He thought doing it on stage while you were performing was going to be this grand gesture.' Kit sighed and moved ahead as the line surged forward. Mrs Higgins came out of the café carrying a coffee and a large blueberry muffin. She stopped in front of Kit and Angela, a mischievous grin on her lined face.

'That was a fabulous show last night, Kit. I'm not sure what part your young beau was supposed to be playing, but it gave us all a laugh. I'll be sure to print my review in next week's newspaper.' Kit groaned, and Angela shook her head. Having hit her target, Mrs Higgins nodded and walked up the road towards the Community Resource Centre, stopping to chat with Mrs Kellerman and Mrs Hopkins. All three women looked back towards the café.

'Trust her to keep the gossip flowing,' Angela said. The line cleared, and they moved up towards the counter. 'Time for something sweet and percolated.'

Coffee and cakes in hand, they walked over to the general store to see Charlotte. Angela filled her in on what was supposed to happen at the concert.

'It all makes sense now. You know what? I didn't want to accept when Kane proposed,' Charlotte said.

Kit and Angela both sat up. 'What? You two are made for each other.' They said in unison. Charlotte laughed.

'It's true. I mean, we were both so young. Mum and Dad loved him, but they were concerned too. Still, it turned out all right in the end. I haven't divorced him yet,' she said loudly as Kane walked through the door. His head jerked towards them, a look of worry etched on his face. 'We're just mucking around,' Charlotte said, before getting up and pecking him on the cheek.

On the drive back to the farm, Kit's mind ruminated on what had happened. Her reaction to Will's news had been out of character. She loved him. Why had she rejected him like that? Did she want to punish him for embarrassing her? Or was it something more? Whatever it was, she wasn't ready to deal with it just yet. She turned the music up and sang at the top of her lungs, letting the music clear her mind.

Chapter 8

Tom

December 24

The cacophony of loud voices and country music hit Tom as he opened the door to the front room of the Imperial Hotel. He looked around before taking a spot at the end of the bar. Shirley plonked a beer in front of him.

'You look like you need it,' she said. He felt like he needed it too. He'd spent the morning mending fences and fixing the oil leak in his old ute. Will had been quiet while they worked. Tom didn't want to pry. He'd been dodging Kit's mood swings for the last day. It was like living with a teenager again. He didn't miss the rows they'd had over what she wore and when her curfew should be. But she'd turned out all right in the end.

'You coming in for Christmas dinner tomorrow night?' Shirley asked. Kit had wanted a family dinner at home this year, just him, her and Will. He shook his head.

'Kit's got it sorted. But I'd love a steak and chips.'

'No worries,' Shirley said, before taking his order through to the kitchen. A familiar scent wafted into his nostrils—lavender and jasmine. He turned to find Cynthia hopping onto the stool next to him. She looked up with a small smile. Tom ordered them both a beer.

'So you're staying in town then?' he asked.

'I'm seriously thinking about it. I think we need to clear the air, though.' Tom froze and kept his eyes on his glass. 'I was hurt when you refused to move away with me. It took me a long time to trust anyone again,' Cynthia said, her voice cracking slightly.

Tom felt nauseous and swallowed the lump in his throat. 'I really am sorry. I just couldn't leave.' Cynthia took a deep breath and blew the air out slowly.

'There has to be more to it than that.' Tom shrugged. Cynthia closed her eyes briefly. 'You know what. I thought I could do this. I thought I could just forgive and forget. But it's a lot harder than I thought it would be.'

'That's it then? You're not going to come back to the Ridge because of me.'

'I was testing the waters by coming back for the fair. They're too cold and deep.' She pushed back off the stool and stood facing him. 'Goodbye, Tom.'

'Cynthia...wait.' She pivoted and was out the door before Tom could get off his stool. He ran outside and looked up and down the street, but couldn't see her. His chest felt tight, and he couldn't get enough air. Putting a hand on his chest, he staggered back and leaned against the wall of the pub. Was he having a heart attack? He closed his eyes and tried to slow his breathing. Eventually, it settled back into its normal rhythm. He went back inside and tried to finish his meal, but his mind wasn't on the food in front of him. It was stuck on an event that happened over forty years ago.

He hadn't told Cynthia back then why he couldn't go with her, but why was he so reluctant to tell her now? Seeing her again had stirred up long-forgotten feelings. She was still as beautiful as she had been when she was younger, and he still felt butterflies in his stomach every time he was near her. Kate had been the love of his life. He'd adored her, and their marriage was a happy one. But she'd been gone for almost fifteen years now. Cynthia was a good woman, and she deserved to know the truth. If he told her the truth, she might stay, and if she stayed, who knew what might happen.

'Hey Shirley, have you got the phone numbers of the stallholders from the fair?'

'Yeah, why's that?'

'You reckon you could give me Cynthia's phone number?' Shirley raised her eyebrows and pursed her lips.

'I can't give out personal information.' She lifted a black notebook from under the bar and placed it on top, tapping it once. 'Oh look, Larry needs a drink.' She headed to the far end of the bar. Tom didn't waste any time. He flipped the pages until he found the schedule for the fair and ran his finger down the list of names until he located Cynthia Douglas.

The phone rang out, so he tried a second time. Cynthia answered on the first ring.

'Cynthia, it's Tom. Don't hang up.' He waited for a response. 'I need to tell you the truth, and it should be in person. Can you meet me at the cemetery gates in fifteen minutes?'

'The cemetery?'

'Trust me.'

Tom walked down the main street. There was no one at the cemetery when he arrived, so he sat on the bench and waited. Minutes later, a silver hatchback pulled up, and Cynthia got out.

'Why on earth are we meeting here?'

'Follow me.' Tom led her through the rows of graves until he found the one he was looking for. He stood in front of it so Cynthia couldn't read the inscription. He hadn't visited in a while. The flowers he'd brought last time were long dead, wilted and decayed.

'What's this all about?' Cynthia asked, hands on her hips, eyebrows knitted together. Tom wrung his hands and then clenched them at his sides.

'I loved you. I wanted to move away with you. To build the life we'd dreamed of. But I couldn't. There wasn't anyone else. At least not romantically.' Cynthia frowned. Tom took a deep breath. 'It was my dad. He was diagnosed with dementia a few weeks before we planned to leave.' Cynthia gasped and put her hand on his arm. He shifted aside, and she read the inscription.

'Oh, Tom. I'm so sorry. Why didn't you tell me?' Tom shrugged.

'He'd been unwell for a while. We ignored it for as long as we could. Put his symptoms down to being busy. By the time we took it seriously, it was close to the end.' Tom's breath hitched, and he coughed to clear his throat. Cynthia looked at the headstone, then closed her eyes and shook her head.

'All these years, I blamed you. I thought you just left me high and dry.' She looked up at him, eyes brimming with tears and regret. 'But you were in an awful situation. I understand why you felt like you couldn't leave.' Tom put his hand in hers and squeezed it gently. She moved closer and lay her head on his shoulder.

'Do you think you might come back to the Ridge now?'

Cynthia hesitated, then looked up at him. 'I think I might.'

'Well, in that case. Would you like to have Christmas dinner with us?' Cynthia beamed, and Tom felt a familiar flutter that had been dormant for many years.

Chapter 9
Kit

December 24

Wind whipped through Kit's hair, and the wide open space of the farm spread out before her. She spotted the dust billowing behind her dad's ute coming up the driveway and galloped to meet him. She leaned down closer and felt her horse's muscles moving in time with the thunderous beat of hooves on the ground. A sense of freedom came over her, and she let out a squeal of delight. Slowing to a trot as she got closer to the house, she rubbed the horse's neck, and it lifted its head up and down, whinnying.

'Looks like you both enjoyed that,' Tom said. Kit dismounted and led the horse into the stables. Tom followed her, helping to unhook the saddle. He hung it on the rack on the wall and turned to face her. Kit knew from his stance that he was about to say something that might upset her. She braced herself. 'I invited Cynthia to lunch tomorrow.'

'You what? Christmas dinner is for family,' Kit said, folding her arms.

'She might not be family, but she is a friend.'

'A good friend, from the sounds of it.' Tom gave her a stern look, and she put her hands up.

'There are a few things I need to tell you. It all happened before I met your mother.' Kit listened as Tom recounted his relationship with Cynthia and why he didn't leave town with her.

'Why didn't you tell her about Granddad back then?' Kit asked. Tom shrugged.

'I thought she would be better off without me. I wasn't in a good headspace. People talk about mental health now, but it wasn't discussed back in those days,' Tom said as they both walked out of the stables. Kit looked over at her dad. He'd been through so many tough experiences: his dad's dementia, losing her mum to cancer. He deserved whatever happiness he could get. Kit stopped walking.

'Dad?' Tom stopped and turned to her, eyes wide. 'Tell Cynthia dinner's at 6.' Kit's heart melted at the look on her father's face.

'I will. And you'd better sort things out with Will.' She laughed and nodded. She knew she was ready to do just that.

The kitchen benches were covered in dishes, Christmas carols blasted from the speaker, and the scent of roast vegetables filled the air. Kit placed the baking tray on the bench, then grabbed the placemats and napkins to finish setting the table. She looked around the room. It was a festive extravaganza. The Christmas tree stood in the corner, lit up and covered in tinsel and decorations. The star she'd made in kindergarten took pride of place on top. Every available surface was covered with Christmas-themed trinkets and knick-knacks that her mother had accumulated over the years. Her father had laughed when he'd walked in and seen the display, and they'd spent some time reminiscing about her mum.

There was a knock on the back door, and Kit turned to see Cynthia standing there in black slacks and a silver top, with silver earrings dangling almost down to her shoulders. She held out a bottle of wine as Kit moved aside to let her in.

'Dad's still getting ready. He hasn't taken this much pride in his appearance in a long time. You must mean a lot to him,' Kit said. Cynthia smiled and smoothed the back of her hair just as Tom came in.

'Cynthia, come in. You look lovely,' he said.

'You've certainly spruced up since I last saw you.' Tom's cheeks coloured.

'Let me formally introduce you to my daughter, Kit. And this,' he pointed towards the back door, 'is her boyfriend, Will.' After the introductions, Tom, Cynthia, and Will took their seats, and Kit brought out the meal. She kept a close eye on Tom and Cynthia's interactions. She realised it had been a long time since she'd seen her dad this happy.

'That was delicious, love. Well done!' Tom said, rubbing his stomach. Will and Cynthia chimed in with their compliments, and Kit felt her chest swell.

Cynthia offered to help clean up. While Will and Tom made their way onto the back verandah, beers in hand, watching the sky change as the sun began to set.

'Thanks for having me here. I know it was meant to be a family thing,' Cynthia said, replacing the tea towel on the hanger.

'No worries. Dad's clearly wrapped to have you here. This is what Christmas is all about. Now, let's grab a drink and join those two before they start talking about cattle again,' Kit said.

The sun was setting, painting the vast sky in bursts of orange and pink. The air was still warm, and the birds squawked loudly as they settled down to roost in the trees near the house. Kit moved closer to Will on the settee and looked across at her dad and Cynthia. They'd barely stopped talking and laughing the entire night. They were like teenagers. Will leaned in close to Kit and whispered, 'Can we go for a walk?' She stood and grabbed his hand, pulling him to his feet. Will led her towards the biggest tree in the paddock closest to the house. They stopped, hands intertwined, and watched the sun dip further. Will squeezed Kit's hand and faced her.

'Kit. You are funny, clever, an amazing singer, and incredibly beautiful. And you are the most precious thing in the world to me.' He put his hand in his pocket and knelt on one knee. 'Katherine Maree Brody, will you marry me?' Kit's breath caught in her throat, and tears streamed down her face.

'Yes,' she said, nodding, and holding out her hand. 'I would love to be your wife. But you have to promise that we're not going to turn into an old, boring couple. Promise we'll still muck around and laugh until our stomachs ache, that we'll dance around the living room, and that we'll never go to sleep fighting again.'

Will held a hand over his heart. 'I promise,' he said, slipping the ring on her finger. She pulled him up, and he wrapped his arms around her. They kissed long and slowly before breaking apart.

'Phew. I'm glad I got it right this time,' Will said, pretending to wipe his brow. Kit nudged him in the side and laughed.

'It was absolutely perfect,' she said. They held each other for a moment, then walked back to the verandah to watch the sun finally set.

✪

Later that night, Kit rolled over and put one leg over Will's, her head on his shoulder, watching his chest rise and fall. He stretched and wrapped his arm around her back, resting it on her waist.

'Geez, I'm glad to have you back beside me again,' he said.

'I don't know how you managed without me,' she joked. Will tickled her gently, eliciting a girly giggle.

'So, where to from here?' he asked.

'The rest of our lives,' Kit replied.

THE END

Courage and Dust

Sanderson Ridge Book 2

Chapter 1

Wet Season

Heavy raindrops pelted down, drenching the cattle huddled in the paddocks and turning the red dirt into a minefield of puddles. Kit pulled on her jacket and slipped her feet into a pair of gum boots, then waited for a break in the rain. When the downpour slowed, she walked over to the shed to find her husband and father. Will and Tom had spent the morning attempting to repair Tom's old ute. He'd owned it since he was in his early thirties and wouldn't dare part with it, even though rust had almost worn a hole in the front floor large enough to see the ground beneath. He'd told Kit once that he felt like he couldn't abandon it after owning it for so long. He probably felt the same way about their farm on the outskirts of Sanderson Ridge. Tom and his late wife Kate had raised Kit on the property, where generations of Tom's family had lived, rearing countless herds of cattle. Kit had learned to drive in the paddocks, sitting on a cushion and grinding the gears of the old ute that Tom was attempting to repair.

Kit stepped inside the shed and shook the water off her jacket, letting her eyes adjust to the dim light. Will was sitting in the driver's seat, waiting for Tom to give him the signal. He turned the key, and the engine spluttered for a moment, then fell silent. He tried again, and it sprang to life. Tom thumped his hand on the bonnet and let out a whoop.

'See. I told you the old girl still had some life left in her,' he said with a satisfied grin. 'I'll be able to pass it on to your little one.'

Kit rubbed her swollen stomach protectively. 'Yeah, right, Dad. I'd prefer my child to drive something with more modern features, like a reliable engine, air conditioning, or even just a working stereo.'

Will laughed as he got out. 'If this kid sings as much as you, it's going to need a decent stereo,' he said, giving her shoulders a quick squeeze. 'Is lunch ready?' he asked. Kit nodded. 'Excellent. I'm starving.'

'You're always starving,' Kit said, then pulled her jacket tighter before heading back to the homestead. It was only fifty metres from the shed, but the rain was so heavy that by the time they reached it, they all looked like drowned rats.

Cynthia, Tom's girlfriend, was wiping the kitchen bench when the group walked in, shaking the water off themselves.

'Look at you lot. I've got just the thing to warm you up,' she said. Tom pecked her on the cheek as he took the plate from her. Kit smiled at their display of affection. Tom had been single for years after Kit's mother died, and even though it was strange at first, Kit had been happy to see Tom reunite with his high school sweetheart. She took her plate and sat next to Will, who was already tucking into the meal.

'Shall we tell them?' Tom said to Cynthia, nodding his head in Kit and Will's direction. Kit's brow furrowed as a bright smile spread across Cynthia's face. They were up to something.

'Tell us what?' Kit asked, stiffening her spine.

Tom cleared his throat with an air of importance. 'You two are about to become a family. You'll need more room. So, we were thinking that you should move in here. We'll take the cottage.'

Kit sat in stunned silence, looking from her father to Cynthia. She hadn't even entertained the thought of moving out of the cosy one-bedroom house on the edge of the farm that she and Will had lived in for a few years. It had been their private love nest while they were dating, and since they had married early last year, it had become their sanctuary from the world. It was the one place they could chill out and be themselves. Admittedly, it was small, but when the baby arrived, he or she could bunk in with them. The baby wouldn't need its own room for a while. In contrast, the homestead had three bedrooms, an office, a large open-plan kitchen, dining and living room, and a wraparound verandah. It was a lovely house. But it was her parents' house.

'We can't do that,' Kit said, shaking her head. She couldn't make her dad move out of the family home. It wouldn't feel right.

'Of course you can. Like your father said, you'll need the extra room when the baby comes. It's just the two of us. We don't need a big house like this. It makes perfect sense,' Cynthia said.

'That's right,' Tom said, nodding. 'It's the best option for everyone.' Kit looked at Will, and he raised his hands in surrender.

'It's up to you, babe,' he said. Kit's eyes wandered around the room. Her amateur artwork from primary school was framed alongside pictures from her childhood, photos of her mum, and newer pictures of her and Will, and Tom and Cynthia.

'Can I think about it?' she asked.

'Sure, you can. But don't leave it too long. You've got a deadline,' Tom said, nodding toward her midsection.

Beth's was bustling with the chatter of customers and clinking of coffee cups. The café had been renovated in a retro theme and had become the go-to spot in Sanderson Ridge for catch-ups. Kit parked her car down the main street near the general store owned by her best friend Angela's sister, Charlotte, and her husband, Kane. It was Charlotte who had completed the renovations, transforming the building from a run-of-the-mill bakery into the thriving café it was now. Spotting Angela and Charlotte standing on the footpath up ahead, Kit called out and jogged to catch up. The three women entered the café and sat at a recently vacated booth by the front window. Lara, the waitress, greeted them and took the empty cups and plates away.

'I'll be back in a minute to take your order,' she said, looking frazzled.

'Take your time. No rush,' Angela said with a smile. Once they were alone, Angela turned to Kit, her hand resting on her stomach. 'So, has your morning sickness passed yet? Mine's finally gone, I hope,' she said, crossing her fingers.

'Yeah, I think so. Although it was more like morning, noon, and night sickness,' Kit said. Angela nodded, lips pursed.

'You two are so cute,' Charlotte said. Angela gave her daggers, and she laughed. 'I just mean it's cool that you were childhood besties and now you're both pregnant at the same time. Your kids are going to grow up together and be besties too.'

'Of course they will,' Kit said, grinning. 'Although I hope they don't get up to quite as much as we did back in the day. Remember that day we tried to catch the bus to Gero and your mum caught us?'

Angela burst out laughing. 'I'd forgotten about that. Good times,' she said, still chuckling. 'Speaking of parents, have you decided what to do about your dad's offer?'

Kit and Will had talked about it many times over the last week. It made sense for them to have the bigger house. They were planning to have more than one child, after all. But Kit was still uneasy about it. 'No. Not yet. It'll feel weird to kick Dad out.'

'You're not kicking him out. He offered you the house. Besides, he'll still be on the farm. It's not like you're making him move into town,' Angela said.

'He wouldn't have offered if he hadn't wanted to do it. You know your dad is as stubborn as you,' Charlotte said. Lara came back to take their order and returned a few minutes later. As they ate, the conversation turned to Angela and Nate's relationship.

'So, do you think he'll propose before the baby comes?' Charlotte asked.

Angela shrugged. 'No idea. We've talked about it, but I told him it wasn't important. We've got too much else to pay for at the moment. We couldn't afford a wedding.'

'It doesn't have to cost much. I'll do all the decorating for free. I'm sure Nate can use the footy clubrooms for free too since he's on the team,' Charlotte said.

Angela shook her head. 'It's not the right time.'

'Suit yourself,' Charlotte said. Her phone buzzed with a reminder notification. 'I've got to go. I'm doing a webinar in half an hour.' Charlotte sculled her drink, waved goodbye, and was out the door before Kit had even finished her chocolate chip muffin.

Driving back through Sanderson Ridge, Kit looked out the windscreen and thought about what Angela had said. She wasn't making her dad move into town. He would have hated that. Nestled in the middle of Western Australia, Sanderson Ridge had a population of just over 2000. It was the major town in the shire and was growing every year. Besides the pub, general store, petrol station, council chambers, community resource centre, and Beth's, the main street now boasted a bookstore packed with the latest releases and a small shop full of quirky decorative items. Ever since Angela and Nate started the station stay, tourism numbers had increased, and some of those tourists had decided to call Sanderson Ridge home. Kit couldn't blame them. With the rocky ridge as a backdrop, the town was picturesque. It had been a great place to grow up. Kit and Angela had always managed to have fun. Whether it was dam swims, riding horses and motorbikes, or causing mischief at the Christmas Fair, growing up in the outback town had been a blast. And now, her own child would get to have the same experiences. Kit contemplated her decision. In her head, she knew it made sense to move into the homestead, but her heart was pulling her in different directions.

✪

Will rolled over and turned the alarm off before it woke Kit. He lay back on the pillow with one arm on his stomach and the other tucked under his head, letting out a soft sigh. With calving season approaching, he knew he was about to get slammed with work. Life on a cattle station was never dull, and an infinite list of tasks awaited Will and his father-in-law every day, but certain times of the year were busier than others. Before she got pregnant, Kit had been a big help, but as the pregnancy progressed, she'd started to take a step back. Some of the local lads helped them during busy months, and now and then, men passing through would work on farms to make some money before they continued their journey. That's how Will had met Kit. He'd been travelling around Australia and had stopped at Sanderson Ridge to work on a farm on the other side of town. One night, not long after he'd arrived, he'd gone to the pub for dinner. He met Kit and fell hard. They'd been together ever since. Now with their first child on the way, Will felt like his life was as perfect as it could get. He felt the mattress shift as Kit snuggled closer to him, laying a hand on his chest.

53

'Morning, sweetheart,' he said, bringing her hand to his lips. She greeted him and then ran her hand down his chest, stomach, and beyond.

Afterwards, they walked hand in hand toward the paddock near the shed, where the heifers were waiting to give birth to their calves. As new mothers, they received extra attention to ensure everything went smoothly. The older, more experienced cows were in a paddock further away. Will pushed open the gate to let Kit through before closing it behind them. Kit made a beeline for the newborn calf standing near its mother, away from the rest of the herd. Will kept his eyes on the cow while Kit bent down to check on the calf.

'This one looks healthy. The herd's expanding rapidly this year,' she said.

'We'll have our work cut out for us. In more ways than one,' Will said, a smile on his face. Kit stood and winced, putting a hand on her lower back. Will's smile faded. 'Are you alright?'

Kit waved him away. 'I'm fine. I've still got a few more months before I'm useless around here.'

'You're never going to be useless. You can mend my clothes while you rest,' he said with a wink. Kit laughed and stood on her tiptoes to kiss him.

'Geez, you're a cheeky bugger, aren't you?'

'That's why you love me,' he said. She took his hand, and they walked around the paddock, checking the rest of the heifers. When they were done, Kit kissed him before heading back to their cottage.

Will lifted his hat and wiped the droplets from his brow, wondering if he'd ever get used to the high humidity that often made him sweat so much his clothes had permanent stains under the armpits. That was something he'd not encountered until he started working up North. Being from the south coast of New South Wales, he hadn't had to deal with it, but as he made his way around Australia, he'd experienced a range of working conditions and a wide variety of jobs. He'd tried working at a brewery in Margaret River, but the number of people who came through during the peak tourist season was enough to put him off hospitality for good. He'd enjoyed working on a dairy farm near Harvey. He liked the quiet little town, but after he'd visited all the local sights, it was time to move further north. He'd enjoyed working for a mechanic in Kalgoorlie for a while before making his way to Sanderson Ridge. Truth be told, if he hadn't met Kit, he'd have moved on by now, but life often takes unexpected turns.

He jumped in the ute and headed out to check the paddocks on the east side of the property. Driving along the fence line, he turned up the radio and sang along, tapping his fingers on the steering wheel. The sky had darkened, and rain threatened again. Something on the ground near the open gate caught his eye. Tom's tool bag was lying on the ground. He knew Tom hadn't been out this way for a few days. Will thought back to when he'd first started working on the farm. He'd bought himself a new tool bag and was showing it off to Tom. The older man shook his head and said, 'Nothing beats something tried and tested like this one right here.' He patted the worn leather tool bag and told Will about his dad, who had worked on the farm his entire life. Tom was always so careful with that bag. Why would he leave it out in the paddock, especially in weather like this?

Will slowed the ute to a stop. Looking around the paddock, there was no sign of any livestock. At least they hadn't got through the opening. He closed and latched the gate, then put the tool bag on the ute tray and drove back towards the homestead.

Tom was standing in the stables brushing one of the horses when Will pulled up outside.

'I found this out near the back paddock,' Will said, holding the tool bag up for Tom to see. Tom's face dropped for a moment before he recovered.

'I was heading back out there today, so I thought I'd leave it,' he said. There was something about his manner that Will couldn't quite put his finger on. Maybe he was stressed about calving season. Will walked over to the bench along the wall.

'Well, I'll just leave it here then,' he said, setting the tool bag down. Tom went back to brushing the horse. Will waited, but Tom didn't offer any further explanation or orders. 'I might head into town and see Kane about those tags. We've had a few new calves today, and there's plenty more on the way, so we'll need them soon.' As Will drove down the long gravel driveway, he couldn't shake the sense of foreboding that had settled in his stomach.

✪

Cynthia sprayed herself with her favourite perfume, then pulled on a black jacket and a green silk scarf. Checking herself in the mirror, she spotted Tom's eyes on her from across the room. She blew him a kiss, then turned around to find him sitting on the bed, buttoning a clean checked shirt and tucking it into his jeans.

'I thought it was the woman who was meant to take a long time getting ready. If you don't get a wriggle on, we're going to be late,' Cynthia teased. Tom stood and pulled her to him.

'They can wait,' he said, bending to kiss her on the forehead as he ran his hands through her short copper hair. Cynthia melted into him for a moment, then gently pushed his chest and took a step back.

'Come on, birthday boy. Let's go celebrate!'

The sandstone Imperial Hotel had brought people together since 1905, and it wasn't slowing down with age. Every table in the restaurant at the side of the pub was full. The noise was an assault on the ears, but Cynthia relished it. She craved being around people. That's why she jumped at the chance to take over the Community Resource Centre when Rose Higgins retired earlier in the year. Rose had found it hard to let go, and they'd clashed when Cynthia tried to put her own stamp on the place. Eventually, Rose caved. Cynthia knew she would. Getting her own way was one of her talents.

As he moved around the table, Tom greeted the guests with a handshake or a hug. Cynthia made her way over to where the waitress stood. After making the arrangements, she sat next to Tom, who had taken his place at the head of the table. As the food made its way out of the kitchen and the drinks were topped up, the atmosphere grew livelier. Cynthia watched Will stagger to the men's room.

'Lucky he's got a designated driver,' she said to Kit.

'For now. As soon as this baby's out, I'll be making up for it,' Kit replied. Cynthia laughed and held her wineglass up in salute before taking a sip.

'So, have you given any more thought to your dad's offer?' Kit shook her head. Cynthia sighed, then looked up as Tom and Will returned to the table. She watched as Tom looked around the room for a moment, then spotted her and took his seat again.

'Everything alright, honey?'

'All good,' Tom replied. Cynthia noted Kit's quizzical expression.

'Your father's been a bit forgetful lately. Too much on his mind, I think.' Tom shifted in his seat, then took a swig of beer, clearly uneasy with the topic of conversation.

'Like leaving your tool bag in the back paddock,' Will said with a chuckle. 'I thought I was seeing things. Luckily, I picked it up before the big downpour.' Tom remained silent. Kit caught Cynthia's eye and pointed her thumb toward the door.

The sky was clear, and the stars were out. The outback night sky never ceased to amaze Cynthia. It was one of the most incredible things she'd ever seen—a million stars dotting the dark canvas like a painting. She took a deep breath and closed her eyes for a moment as Kit caught up with her. Opening her eyes, she found Kit leaning on the windowsill, her eyebrows knitted together and her mouth in a thin line.

'What's going on with Dad?' Kit said. She never bothered with preamble, but Cynthia would have liked more time to consider how to deal with Kit's probing.

'He's just been preoccupied lately, that's all. I've been trying to convince him to make a doctor's appointment, but you know what he's like,' Cynthia said, shrugging a shoulder. Like most men, especially country men, Tom didn't like to dwell on any possible medical issues. She guessed the thinking behind it was that if they ignored the problem, it would go away.

'You need to make it for him then,' Kit said, folding her arms.

'I will. I promise. Let's get back in there and get him to open his presents. I'm dying for him to see what I got him,' Cynthia said, brimming with anticipation. She watched Kit put a hand on the wall and push herself off. She looked tired. She didn't need to worry about what was going on with her father. Becoming a mum for the first time was enough of a change.

Back at the table, Will, Tom, Kane, and Nate were deep in discussion about the last televised cricket match. Cynthia rolled her eyes at Angela, then gently clinked a knife against her wineglass. She remained still, waiting patiently for everyone's gaze to shift in her direction.

'Thank you all for coming to celebrate Tom's birthday. We all know he's a stoic man who adores his family and doesn't like the attention being on himself. I told him that was just too bad because we all wanted an excuse to celebrate, and he was it.' Enthusiastic cheers erupted from everyone at the table. Cynthia smiled and waited a moment, then turned to Tom. 'I wanted to get you something special,' she said, handing him an envelope. Tom took it and tried to put it on the table.

'Open it,' Kane and Will called out. Cynthia nodded and watched eagerly as Tom ripped the end of the envelope open and pulled out the pieces of paper. His jaw dropped as he realised what he was holding. Cynthia felt a surge of excitement run through her body.

'I can't accept this,' Tom said, shaking his head.

'What is it, Dad?' Kit asked. Tom turned it around to show the group the plane tickets to England. Kit's face mirrored her father's while everyone around them clapped and cheered. Cynthia bent to kiss Tom on the cheek.

'You've always wanted to go back and see where your ancestors came from. Now you can. The tickets are variable, so we can travel when it suits us. After Kit is settled in with the baby, of course.'

'It's too much, sweetheart.'

'You deserve it,' Cynthia said. It would be an amazing holiday, and it would give Tom something to focus on. Hopefully, that would ease some of the frustration he'd been feeling lately, and things could return to normal.

Chapter 2

Kit was sprawled on the couch when Will emerged from the bathroom after washing the dirt of the day away. She lifted her head so he could sit in his favourite spot, then she laid her head back down on his lap. He ran his hand through her dark hair as they watched the reporter standing outside Parliament relaying the latest drama during Question Time. Kit sighed as the adverts started.

'What's up?'

Kit turned to look up at him. 'I think we should take Dad and Cynthia up on their offer.'

'Is this your final decision?' he asked, eyebrows raised. They'd had this exact conversation multiple times, and each time Kit had changed her mind. 'You know I don't care either way.' Kit pursed her lips.

'Maybe…'

Will chuckled. 'Well, we've still got a few months before we have to worry about it. Oh, I forgot to tell you. Nate and I are heading up to the ridge tomorrow after work. You should hang out with Angela.'

'Nah. I think I'll stay home. The cottage needs a good clean.'

'Who are you and what have you done with my wife?'

'What?'

'You hate cleaning?'

Kit shrugged. 'Maybe it's that nesting phase I read about.' Will leaned down and kissed her forehead, then her lips.

'There's another part of this trimester that might interest you,' she said with a smirk before reaching up and gently tugging his earlobes, sending a shiver down his body. This pregnancy thing isn't all bad, he thought as he lifted her up and maneuvered her body on the couch.

The sun was low in the sky, and the puddles were drying, but the weather report had said more storms were on the way later in the week. Will kicked his leg, and the motorbike sprang to life. He revved it a few times before clicking it into gear. The wind whipped through his hair as he left a wavy skid in the gravel driveway. The motorbike wasn't as handy as the ute, but it was more fun to zip through the paddocks to get to Ridgeview, Angela and Nate's farm. Nate still owned Fonty Downs, the farm that stood between the Brody farm and Ridgeview Station, so it didn't matter that Will snuck through the back paddocks from time to time. Desmond and Daisy Jurrah managed Fonty Downs for Nate, and they were the most laid-back couple you could meet. When Will reached Ridgeview, he found Nate standing on the driveway near his motorbike.

'You took your time,' he chided.

'Had to check on the heifers. A few of them are ready to drop,' Will answered.

'I've got a couple of drinks,' Nate said, patting the bag strapped to the back of the motorbike. 'Let's crack on.' They rode off with Nate's dog, Bizkit, and Angela's dogs, Josie and Pippa, in tow. The dogs kept up with the bikes as they raced down the track past the one-bedroom silo and two-bedroom dongas that Nate and Angela rented out to tourists. Nate waved at a couple sitting on the deck of a donga, relaxing and watching the sun make its way down towards the ridge.

The two men parked their motorbikes and raced each other to climb up to a ledge that faced back towards Ridgeview and the farms beyond. Will reached the ledge first and let out a triumphant yell before settling on the warm rock. Nate handed him a beer and cracked one open for himself. Will leaned back on a rock and took a swig of beer.

'How's the serenity?' he said. Nate nodded. They sat in silence for a few moments, watching the colours of the land change as the sun slowly lowered.

'How's Desmond going at Fonty Downs?' Will asked. Desmond and Daisy Jurrah's connection to the land was extraordinary. Will guessed that happened when your people had lived there for thousands of years.

'It's thriving. He and Daisy have got that place running like a well-oiled machine. Desmond found an underground well that I never even knew was on the property,' Nate said with an impressed grin.

'Nice. How's Ang going with the pregnancy? Kit's been so moody lately. It's to be expected, I suppose.'

'Yeah, true. I can't wait to be a dad, though. I reckon I'm more excited about it than Ang.'

Will laughed. 'Me too. I reckon Kit's having a boy.'

Nate shrugged. 'I'll be happy either way.'

'Yeah. Same. Here's to good things ahead,' Will said, holding up his beer. They clinked bottles and relaxed back on the rocks.

When the sun was hitting the horizon, and their stomachs started growling, they climbed back down. The dogs, who'd been dozing nearby, started watching the men, waiting for the moment the motorbikes would take off so they could prove their running ability. Turning the throttle and revving the engine, Will rode ahead. With any luck, Kit would have dinner for him when he got home. He glanced back to check where Nate and the dogs were. Nate gave him the finger, and he laughed. Rotating to the front, he squinted in the fading light. Was that a rabbit or a tuft of grass? He couldn't make out a lot. A rock had broken the headlight on his dirt bike the last time he'd ridden it. He'd meant to fix it, but there were more important things to do. A dark shadow flashed in front of him, and the bike started wobbling. As he tried to steady it, the front wheel hit a deep pothole in the track. Time slowed to a crawl as his body flew over the handlebars, landing with a thud and terrifying crack. The bike, still revving, swerved uncontrollably, flipped, and landed on top of him. The smell of oil and fuel filled his nostrils, and the heat from the engine seared his skin. As unbearable pain surged through his body, Will felt his head loll to the side before everything went black.

★

The bass thumped through the cottage walls and floor. Kit folded the shirt in her hands and sang along at the top of her lungs. She might be a domestic goddess in training, but she could still belt out a tune. She picked up a pile of Will's shirts and pants and headed for their bedroom, dancing over the vacuum that she'd forgotten to put away earlier. She came back out and picked the vacuum wand up, singing the song's final words into the hole at the end of the pipe. The house fell silent for a moment before Kit heard someone pounding on the front door.

'Hold your horses,' she called as she walked down the hallway. 'What's the emergency?' she said, rolling her eyes as she opened the door. Her face paled as she saw the look on Angela's face. Kit grabbed the doorframe as her body stiffened. 'What's going on?' she asked. Angela pulled her into the living room and sat her on the lounge. A hard knot formed in Kit's stomach, and she held her breath.

'It's Will,' Angela said. Kit felt the room spin. 'He's been in an accident. Nate was with him. The ambos should be there by now, and the flying doctors are on their way.' Kit stood up and wobbled slightly. Angela held her arms to steady her.

'Is he...? Will he be alright?' Kit's voice was jagged as her breath came in short bursts.

Angela shook her head. 'I don't know. I'm sorry.'

Tears welled in Kit's eyes, and her lips trembled. Her hand flew to her stomach. 'I need to go. I need to be with him.'

Angela nodded. 'I know. I can drive you.'

'I have to tell Dad and Cynthia. I need to...my handbag...I need...'

'It's alright, hun. Just sit for a second. I'll grab your handbag and some clothes for you both.' Kit felt numb as she watched Angela leave the room. This didn't feel real. How could Will be hurt? She'd only seen him a few hours ago. He was fine. Surely, he was fine. Maybe everyone was overreacting. Better safe than sorry, that sort of thing.

Angela ran around from the driver's side to open the passenger door. Kit blinked a few times and looked around. She didn't remember leaving the cottage, let alone getting into the car, and now they were at Ridgeview. Several cars were scattered across the paddock. The flashing ambulance lights painted streaks of red across the twilight sky. Voices were shouting, but Kit couldn't make sense of what they were saying. It was as if everything around her was happening in some kind of alternate reality. Angela gently tugged Kit's arm, and she followed her to the back of the ambulance. Will was strapped to a bed on one side, with an ambulance officer checking the monitor above his head. Kit felt numb. Her mind was both a whirlwind and a void.

'Kit's here,' Angela said. The medic looked up, and Kit realised it was Dave from the footy team. He tried to give her what she assumed was a reassuring smile, but he couldn't hide the worry in his eyes as he helped her up into the back of the ambulance. Angela put the bags under the seat and leaned close to Dave. 'I think she's in shock. Can you check on her? We don't want anything to happen to the baby,' Angela said in a low whisper.

Dave nodded. 'We'll look after them both, Ang,' he said as he shut the back door. The shrill noise of the commotion outside was diluted to just the beeping of machines. Kit looked at Will's sleeping form and reached across to put a hand on his chest. His body was covered with a clean white sheet and thermal rug, but a blood-stained sheet lay on the floor. Dave kicked it under the bed.

'We've bandaged him up, given him painkillers, and sedated him. The flying docs will get him to Perth in no time.' He cleared his throat. 'Do you mind if I do your obs, Kit?' She looked at him, not registering his words. 'I just need to make sure you're both alright.' He looked down at her stomach, and Kit laid a hand across it protectively.

'Oh, right? Of course,' she said, leaning back in the seat. Dave nodded and gave her the once-over, checking her pupils, pulse, breathing, and blood pressure before checking the baby's heartbeat. He sat back in the chair and strapped on his seatbelt.

'You're in a bit of shock, but that's to be expected. We'll just keep an eye on all three of you,' he said with a small smile. Kit's eyes drew back to Will's face. He had the boyish look that took over when he was asleep. Aside from the bloody sheet on the floor, there was no sign that anything was wrong. Dave had discarded the evidence well.

'Will he be alright?' Kit asked.

'He's got a few cuts and burns from the bike landing on top of him. His arm's in a bad way, and they'll need to do further testing to check for spinal injuries.' Kit bit her lip, and Dave laid a hand on her arm. 'We got to him quickly, and the docs in Perth know what they're doing.' Kit nodded and sat back, closing her eyes and trying to steady her breath. There was nothing they could do but wait.

The aeroplane was waiting at Sanderson Ridge's small airport when they arrived. Dave and the other ambulance crew transferred Will to the aeroplane. Kit breathed a sigh of relief when the doctor in charge allowed her to fly with him. Tom and Cynthia had called her to let her know they'd drive down to Perth. Inside the aeroplane, machines beeped, and the doctors and nurses spoke in hushed voices. Kit looked out the window at the dark sky. Before he'd left the house to hang out with Nate, Will had kissed her stomach and then kissed her forehead. It was a moment in time that Kit hadn't realised would be the end of life as they knew it. What would happen now? Would Will have spinal damage or brain damage? What if he couldn't use his arm for a while? How was he supposed to work? How were they supposed to deal with all this so close to becoming a family? Kit closed her eyes and let a tear slide down her cheek. As much as she tried not to worry, she knew this night was going to be one of the toughest she and Will had to face together.

The drive to Perth afforded Cynthia plenty of time to go over the events of the last few hours. She had been about to close the CRC when Tom rang with a tremor in his voice that belied his concern. She'd driven towards Ridgeview, not quite keeping to the speed limit. Tom would chastise her if he knew, especially given how his best friend Jack and his wife Susan had died, but all she'd wanted to do was to be by his side, to help him and Kit in any way she could. She'd arrived at the accident scene just as the ambulance was leaving with Will and Kit inside. Tom was standing next to his old ute. She put her arms around Tom's neck and let him hide his face in her shoulder. He'd been sketchy with the details on the phone, but as they stood with their heads together, he filled her in on what had happened. Angela and Nate had been talking with Constable Mawson. Nate was as white as a sheet as he answered the questions Mawson was throwing at him. Tom had whispered, 'Thanks, love,' before they walked back towards the car. Angela caught up with them.

'I asked Dave to check on Kit,' Angela said.

'Thanks, Ang. Did he say anything else about Will?' Cynthia asked. Angela shook her head, swallowing hard.

'We're going to get our stuff together and head down to Perth,' Tom said.

'Be careful. Make sure you stop somewhere and rest.'

'Will do,' Tom said, squeezing her shoulder. 'We'll keep you updated.'

It hadn't taken them long to pack. They'd stopped in at the cottage to grab some more clothes for both Will and Kit before they'd headed off. They had taken turns driving and resting. It was still dark when they reached the city. Angela's two-bedroom house sat across from a dark, empty park. Cynthia was grateful that Angela's tenant had moved out a few weeks earlier. They dropped their bags on the floor, then headed to the main bedroom. Cynthia knew she wouldn't get to sleep straight away, but after the long drive, Tom was snoring within minutes. She shifted to her other side. Her mind raced, and she picked up her phone to search for a potential diagnosis of motorbike accident injuries. When her eyes began to droop, she placed her phone on the bedside table, hoping that it wouldn't ring again.

The pungent scent of disinfectant assaulted their nostrils as the hospital doors slid open. Tom led the way to the reception desk and asked for Will Stone's room. The receptionist eyed them for a second before checking her computer and giving them Will's room number. They walked through the quiet corridors, their footsteps echoing on the linoleum floor until they came to the right room. Tom halted outside, unsure whether he should enter. Cynthia rubbed his back and then gently opened the door. The room was dark except for the lights emanating from the machinery near the bed Will was sleeping in. Kit was dozing on a fold-out bed by the window. Cynthia tiptoed over, then looked back at the door and frowned. Tom was still standing in the doorway. She motioned for him to come in, and he shook his head for a second.

'He doesn't like hospital rooms,' Kit whispered. Cynthia jolted and looked down to see Kit staring up at her.

'We didn't mean to wake you,' Cynthia said.

'It's okay. I wasn't asleep, anyway.' Her eyes darted towards Will, then settled on Tom. 'It's alright, Dad. Come in.' Tom forced his body forward and came to stand next to Cynthia, while Kit sat up and pulled on a jumper. The monitors surrounding Will's bed beeped and buzzed at regular intervals. No wonder Kit looked like she'd hardly slept.

'How's Will?' Tom asked. Kit's lip quivered, and Tom pulled her into a hug. 'What is it, love? What's happened?' In between sobs, Kit told them everything that had happened since they'd arrived at the hospital. Will had been assessed and then sent straight to surgery. Kit had waited hours for news, and when it came, she felt as if she'd been dealt a blow.

'The doctor said his cuts and burns should heal well. They ran a bunch of tests, but thankfully, the scans don't show any signs of brain or spinal damage.'

'That's fantastic news. So, he'll be alright then?' Tom asked.

Kit shook her head. 'No, Dad. He won't. The nerves in his arm were crushed and severed. The doctors did everything they could, but...' She closed her eyes and shook her head as if she didn't believe what she was about to say. 'He's lost movement in his right arm. They don't think it will ever come back. They said something about the severed nerves stopping the signals from the brain,' Kit said, shaking her head again. 'It was so technical. I just couldn't take it all in.'

Cynthia sucked in a breath and looked at Will. His body was covered with a sheet, with only his head and shoulders showing. There was nothing to show the damage he'd suffered. He'd be devastated when he woke up and realised what had happened. This was going to impact them both for the rest of their lives.

Tom hugged Kit tighter. 'It's alright, love. We'll get through it. He's alive, and that's the main thing, right?' Tom said.

Kit's face clouded. 'He and Nate were drinking up on the ridge. Why the hell would Nate let him ride like that?' she said, anger warbling the edges of her words.

'Will's a man, love. He makes his own choices. Nate told the police that he saw an emu run in front of them, then Will's front wheel hit a pothole and sent him flying. It was an accident. A terrible accident. It was nobody's fault.' Kit sank down onto the bed, her face in her hands. Tom pulled a chair up to the side of Will's bed. Cynthia looked from father to daughter. She felt superfluous. She loved Tom and Kit more than anything in the world, and she couldn't do anything to take away their pain. But she could keep them nourished.

'How about we get some breakfast,' she said to Kit, holding out a hand to help her up. Kit looked at Will. 'I'm sure they'll let us know if he wakes up.'

They sat at a table in the quiet cafeteria, hands wrapped around coffee cups. Cynthia didn't fill the silence, although she wanted to. Talking helped her process things, but she knew Tom and Kit didn't operate the same way. She took a sip of coffee and looked across the cafeteria. How would Kit and Will cope? Would Kit be strong enough to handle it? Kit was resilient, but this was a blow none of them saw coming. And Will, how was this going to impact his life? Cynthia braced herself as Kit let out a sob.

'I can't believe it. It all happened so fast,' she said. 'I feel like one minute he was saying goodbye and heading out

the door, and the next he was in the back of an ambulance.'
Cynthia rested her hand on Kit's arm and squeezed it gently
as she continued. 'How am I going to tell him about the
accident? How am I going to tell him his arm won't work
properly ever again? He's going to be devastated.'

'I know, but we'll get through it. You know what they
say. True strength and love reveal themselves in times like
this,' Cynthia said. 'Your dad and I will support you in any
way we can.' Kit sighed heavily. They finished their coffee in
silence, both contemplating what lay ahead.

Male voices filtered down the corridor. Cynthia
looked across at Kit. The younger woman looked frightened.
Cynthia linked an arm through hers, and they walked into the
room together. Tom was still in the chair beside the bed. Will
had his eyes open, but he was looking past Tom to the
window. He glanced at them with a blank stare on his face.
Standing behind Tom, Cynthia rested a hand on his
shoulder. Kit tentatively touched Will's left arm. He flinched,
and she drew her hand back.

'Will?'

'Sorry,' he said, his voice clipped with emotion.
Cynthia shifted from one foot to the other, a queasy feeling
settling in her stomach.

'We might leave you to it,' she said, nudging Tom.
Out in the corridor, she folded her arms as a shiver ran
through her. The ambient temperature was a steady 24
degrees. It was the idea of what was to come that sent her
cold.

Chapter 3

The homestead was in sight. He glanced back, trying to gauge his lead over Nate, laughing when his mate gave him the finger. He faced forward. A dark shadow crossed the road and...Will woke up, gasping, sweat beading on his brow. His eyes scanned the room. It took a second for the realisation of where he was to filter through his consciousness and a second longer to register the pain that radiated from various parts of his body. His arm and chest were bandaged; his leg ached, and his shoulder throbbed. He couldn't remember ever being in this much pain before. The urge to urinate kicked in, and with a groan, he attempted to push himself up off the bed. His mind thought about the movement he needed to make, but his body failed him. His arm would not move. It lay limp on the bed. He glared at it and cursed as a nurse came in.

'Sorry about that,' he said, cheeks reddening.

'No need to apologise. Can I help with anything?' the nurse asked. Will shook his head. He lay back on the pillow and submitted to her routine observations and accepted the painkillers she offered. But when she left, he hauled himself out of bed and, after relieving himself, hobbled over to the window. The streets below were buzzing with morning traffic; people were heading to work, parents were dropping kids off at school, and everyone was going about their lives. And he was stuck in a hospital room with a shoddy arm that would never work again. He thought back to when Kit had broken the news to him. He'd tried to be stoic. Tom and Cynthia had left the room, and Kit had sat on the side of the bed, tears streaming down her face. He'd said it could have been worse. And it could have. Much worse. But that didn't make it any easier to deal with. The fact remained that his dominant arm was now useless. While Kit cried, his body tensed, and he shut himself off. She didn't need to see him break down. She needed him to be tough, to handle it as a man should. He heard a commotion and turned as Kit waddled through the door with breakfast in a paper bag.

'Morning, did they say you can come home today? You've been in here almost a week already.' Kit said, pecking him on the cheek.

'The doc hasn't been in yet,' Will replied, shuffling back to the bed. 'But even if I can leave, what's going to happen when I go home? I can't work, I can't help you around the house, I can't even bloody dress myself anymore.'

'The nurses have said that you will do all of those things. In time,' Kit said. Her smile was bright, but it didn't reach her eyes.

Will clenched his fist and punched the bed. 'I went from being a man to a bloody cripple overnight. They might as well have taken my arm off. I'd rather that than have it hanging there like a limp reminder of how much I fucked things up.'

'Will,' Kit was about to say more when Doctor Pataki appeared in the doorway. Will shifted in the bed, trying to suppress his rage.

'You're up. Good. How are you feeling today?' The doctor picked up the chart from the holder and scanned the notes. Will thought about how to answer the question. He'd had enough of being in the hospital, and the doctors couldn't do much more for him, anyway. He was going to have to deal with this on his own at some point. He might as well get on with it.

'All good. I guess,' he replied a little tersely. The doctor looked from Will to Kit, then back down at the clipboard.

'Well, everything looks to be in hand. Those cuts and burns will take time to heal. I'll write up some notes for your GP about possible rehabilitation programs, and they can take it from there.' Doctor Pataki smiled at them both. 'Best of luck,' he said, then walked out the door and into the next room to see his next patient. Kit ran after him. Will stood and opened the small closet in the corner of the room. He picked up his bag and dumped it on the bed, then shoved his clothes inside. He went to lift it, cursing as it slipped from his grasp.

'Let me do it,' Kit said, rushing back into the room.

'I can do it myself. I'm not an invalid,' Will said.

'I know. I just—'

'Leave it.' Will bent to pick up the bag and then stalked out the door, his flaccid arm flopping at his side, his frustration boiling to the surface.

The drive back to Sanderson Ridge proved to be as tedious as Will knew it would be. He might have been physically present, but mentally, he was back on his motorbike, keeping his eyes on the road in front of him. He wore headphones for as long as he could, but he knew there would come a point where he'd have to participate in the conversation. Cynthia tried to make small talk, but the elephant in the car was too big to ignore.

'Did you hear me?' Kit asked, putting a hand on his leg.

'Sorry. What?' Will said, pulling down his headphones. She was staring at him, eyes wide, and biting her bottom lip. She'd said something important, and he'd missed it.

'I told Dad and Cynthia we'd take the homestead.'

'Rightio.' Will felt Tom's eyes on him in the rear-view mirror, and he cleared his throat. 'That's good.' What else was he supposed to say? It didn't bother him which house they were in. It wasn't as if he was going to be much help around the house anyway.

When Tom pulled up at the cottage, Kit was quick to grab both of their bags. Will thanked them for going down to Perth. They assured him it was no trouble. Then they drove off toward the homestead, but not before exchanging a glance that Will didn't miss. Kit was in the bedroom, unpacking. Alone in the kitchen, Will looked out the window that faced the driveway. He groaned as the ache in his shoulder returned. The painkillers had worn off, and he needed a top-up. He grabbed a glass and tried to turn on the tap. The glass slipped from his hand, but he caught it before it landed in the sink. He snorted. What a joke! He couldn't even get a glass of water without messing it up. He lobbed back two tablets, waiting for the numbness they'd bring.

His body needed rest, but Will couldn't stay asleep any longer. Every time he moved, the bandage on his burns twitched, and a sharp, stinging pain shot through his shoulder. He opened his eyes and looked around. He was in the living room, not the bedroom. When had he come out here? Had he been sleepwalking? He'd never done it before. Maybe it was a side effect of the medication. Kit's keys were missing from the board near the back door. Relieved, he downed a pill and checked the fridge for whatever was easy to prepare. He popped his head up over the fridge door at the sound of knocking. Nate stood in the doorway, hat in hand, and mouth turned down. Will groaned. He hadn't seen or spoken to Nate since the moment right before the accident. He would have preferred not to see anybody, the way his head was aching, but Nate had already spotted him.

'Hey,' Nate said, hovering near the door.

'Hey,' Will replied, shuffling to take a seat at the dining table. Nate remained standing.

'How are you? I mean...are you alright?' Nate asked. He shook his head and gulped loudly before continuing. 'I just...damn, this is hard.'

Will gazed at him, his expression unreadable. This was hard for him? It wasn't as if he was the one who was maimed in the accident. How the hell did he think Will felt?

'I'm sorry. I feel awful about what happened,' Nate said, eyes down.

Will sighed heavily. 'It happened. Nothing we can do about it now.'

'Yeah, but if I—' Nate started. Will put his hand up to stop him. If only they hadn't gone up the ridge. If only they hadn't been drinking. If only he hadn't looked back. If only the track didn't have potholes. There were so many mitigating factors in the accident, but it had been just that, an accident. He should say more, but there was a part of him that wanted Nate to suffer. It wasn't reasonable or rational thinking, but he couldn't change how he felt. Nate stood there for another minute, then pulled out his phone to check the time. 'I should get going.'

'Catch you later then,' Will said. He didn't bother getting up. He sat at the table, staring out the back door towards the paddocks. His mind felt cloudy. He kept replaying the accident. It shouldn't have happened. But it wasn't Nate's fault. Then again, Nate had walked away that afternoon fully intact. Will was now a cripple.

With a grunt and a muttered curse, Cynthia attempted to lift her end of the roll of wire. If she hadn't checked in with Tom before she'd left for work, she wouldn't be standing in the driveway with arms that felt like they were about to snap. It had been two weeks since the accident. Will was still coming to terms with his disability, and Kit couldn't lift anything heavy in her condition. If she didn't help Tom with this, he'd probably hurt himself trying to do it on his own.

'Almost there,' Tom said as Cynthia struggled to lift the roll higher. Together, they waddled over to the back of the ute. 'Up a bit higher, love,' Tom called out. Puffing out her cheeks, she dropped her end onto the tray and watched the wire roll into the middle. She had to broach the subject of help, but she knew it was going to be a sore point.

'I think we need to get someone in. Just in the interim,' she said. Tom fiddled with the side of the ute tray. 'I know it's not ideal, but we don't know how long it's going to take Will to get a handle on things. And when he does, he won't be able to do what he used to do.'

Tom looked down at his dirty boots while Cynthia waited for his response. Finally, he looked up at her. 'You're right. I'll ask Nate if he knows someone,' Tom said. She pumped her fist as she followed him back into the shed. At least she wouldn't have to work two jobs for much longer.

'Right, Katie. One more to go,' Tom said. Cynthia froze and stared at him, mouth agape.

'What?' he asked with a puzzled expression.

'You just called me Katie.'

'I did not,' he said, shaking his head.

'Yes. You did,' Cynthia insisted, a knot forming in her stomach. He turned away from her, but not before she saw shock register on his face.

'Well, it was a slip of tongue,' Tom huffed over his shoulder. He picked up another roll of wire and waited for her to grab the other end. His jovial demeanour was gone, replaced by unspoken words that hung in the air between them. Cynthia wondered if this latest slip should be added to the growing list of faux pas that were becoming harder to ignore.

Cynthia took a long, slow breath as she pulled up outside the house that was now the Sanderson Ridge Community Resource Centre. Along with access to government services, the centre had public computers and printers, and Cynthia was working on setting it up as a training college. The social groups were another drawcard for people that Cynthia had built up over the last few months. The ladies' craft group was thriving, as was the playgroup. The never-ending to-do list was something Cynthia loved about running the place. She walked around to the front of the building to find Rose Higgins sitting on the bench near the door. As Cynthia approached, Rose made a show of looking at her watch. Ignoring the gesture, Cynthia smiled and unlocked the door, allowing the older woman to enter first.

While Rose busied herself getting the craft items set up on the table in the front room, Cynthia went into her office. She had her head down in paperwork when she heard a knock. Rose stood in the doorway.

'I just wanted to let you know we've finished. Here's the room hire fee,' she said, putting an old tin on the desk. Cynthia glanced at the clock at the bottom of the screen. The morning had got away from her.

'Thanks. Will you be back for choir tomorrow night?'

'Most likely. How are things on the farm?' Rose asked, eyebrows raised. Cynthia knew the question would come, but the last thing the family needed was for Rose to write an article for the local newspaper claiming that the Brody farm was in dire straits. It was better to set the record straight.

'Everyone's fine, and we've got things under control,' she answered. Rose's eyebrows didn't drop as she stood waiting for more. Cynthia kept the forced smile on her face. The older woman wanted gossip, but she wouldn't get much from her. 'And we're looking forward to meeting our first grandchild,' she said, smiling even wider. Rose eyed her for a moment, sensing that Cynthia would not give her anything she could use.

'That's good. I'll see you on time tomorrow night, then,' she said as she turned to leave. Cynthia let her breath out in a puff. The news of Will's accident had been all over town within hours, but if she could keep busybodies like Rose away, then perhaps her family could concentrate on getting through the ordeal without interference.

✪

Overstuffed packing boxes filled the main living area; pieces of discarded tape were scattered on the table, and Kit sat on the floor in the middle of it all, rethinking her decision. Who knew that moving down a driveway would be almost as stressful as moving to a different town? She'd spent the last week going through her possessions, discarding some, carefully packing others. The boxes were filled with everything she'd accumulated since she'd moved from the main homestead to the little cottage when she was eighteen. She'd wanted space then. Not room capacity, but space from the trauma of seeing her mum battling cancer and losing the fight, and of seeing her dad trying to piece together a life without the woman he'd been married to for over twenty years. It had been the toughest year of Kit's life, but having the cottage to retreat to had been a silver lining in the darkest days.

Now in her thirties, she was moving back into the family home. Albeit to start her own family. But even that wasn't going according to plan. Her pregnancy had been textbook so far, but Will's accident hadn't been in their vision for the future. Three weeks had passed since they'd arrived back from Perth, and he'd barely said a word to her. He was clearly in pain. The medication seemed to help, but it also made him less coherent and drowsy. He'd spent most of the day dozing on the couch while Kit packed the last of their belongings. She looked over to find him staring at her. She smiled, and he returned the gesture before his expression morphed into the zoned-out look he'd been wearing lately.

'I think we're ready to go,' Kit said, using the couch to push herself to a standing position. Will used his left arm to launch himself up, then swung his legs to the floor. They stood face to face. Kit waited for a shoulder squeeze or a forehead kiss; anything that would indicate he loved her like he used to. Her body deflated as he walked away. Will returned with a bag over his left shoulder and a small box hugged to his chest. He stopped short when he reached the back sliding door. Kit could almost see the frustration emanate from him like a vapour. She picked up a small box off the coffee table and moved in front of him, opening the door to let him through.

'You're welcome,' she said, her voice dripping with sarcasm. Will harrumphed, then strode to his ute and dropped the box on the tray before shimmying the bag off his shoulder. Anger boiled inside Kit, and she planted herself squarely in his path. 'You need to stop doing this.'

'Doing what?' Will baulked.

'Getting angry when you can't do things the way you used to.'

'Are you kidding me? How do you think it feels to be like this? To be useless.'

'You're not useless. So, your right arm doesn't work. So what? You're alive. You can still walk, talk, and do most of the things you used to do. It's just different now.'

'Yeah. Different for me. But everyone else gets to go on as if nothing happened,' Will spat, eyes narrowed. Kit braced for more vitriol to spill from him, but a moment later, he moved aside and stalked back into the house. If he could be stubborn, then so could she. Kit stormed into the house to grab another box. They loaded the ute and the back of Kit's car in silence.

It was a long afternoon, but with the items from the cottage now in the homestead and vice versa, Kit sat on the back verandah mindlessly scrolling on her phone. Will had spoken with her cursorily while Tom and Cynthia were in earshot, but from the looks that Kit saw pass between them, they'd clearly picked up on the tension. As always, Tom had given her a "She'll be right" speech. Cynthia had chosen not to mention it at all. Kit didn't know which was better. Her phone buzzed.

You up for a mocktail?-Angela texted.

Heck yes-Kit replied.

Taking a long, slow sip, Kit wished she weren't pregnant and that the drink was alcoholic. She could do with something to calm her nerves and help her relax. Meditation didn't do it for her, and she'd never been good at keeping a journal. Angela sat forward, her head cocked to the side.

'You look stressed. Spill,' she said. Kit groaned.

'Is it that obvious?' she asked. Angela's eyebrows shot up, and Kit raised her hands in surrender. 'Alright. I've just had a crappy day, that's all.'

'Was it the move?'

'Yeah. Sort of,' Kit said, twirling the glass in her hand. 'Will's been a bit standoffish lately. To be honest, I'm struggling with it all.'

Angela sat back, her hands on her stomach. 'That's understandable. It's only been a few weeks. He's probably still adjusting.'

'I get that, but does he have to take his frustration out on me?' Kit said. Angela's mouth set in a line.

'Is he hurting you?'

'Gosh, no. Nothing like that. He's been moody, and when he does, it ends in an argument.' Kit took another sip. 'I know I'm not a ray of sunshine. I'm getting tired more easily lately. It feels like I have a basketball in my stomach. What if Will's changed his mind about all this? About me?' Kit said, biting her bottom lip.

Angela got up and came around to Kit's side of the table, then leaned down and hugged her. 'I really don't think that's the case. You just need to give him time. Maybe he should talk to the doctor about what's happening.' Kit swallowed the lump in her throat. She wanted more than anything for Angela to be right.

Later that night, lying in bed next to Will, Kit listened for his steady breathing. A sob escaped her lips. Will rolled to the side, facing her. He reached out and laid a hand on her stomach.

'Is everything alright?' he whispered. Kit closed her eyes. She desperately wanted to say yes, but how could she? Everything was not alright, and she wasn't sure that it would be again. She turned over to face him.

'I think you should speak to the doctor,' Kit whispered, almost afraid to say it.

'What for?' Will moved back slightly.

'Because you seem like you're a bit down.'

'Of course I am. My arm's stuffed, and the painkillers don't work.' A lump formed in Kit's throat. How could she respond to that without turning this into another argument?

'Okay. Goodnight,' she said, faking a yawn as she turned over before he could see the tears that had pricked her eyes.

Chapter 4

As the video played, the computer screen lit up with images of the Tower of London, the London Eye, and the Houses of Parliament, with Big Ben towering in the foreground. Cynthia sighed and clicked out of the video and back to her document. She and Tom had planned to visit England after Kit had her baby, but since Will's accident, everything had changed. They barely had enough time to go to Geraldton, let alone the other side of the world. Pushing back the chair, Cynthia went to the kitchen and made herself a cup of tea. After a quick phone call from Charlotte about the upcoming joint baby shower, she walked down the hallway to the front room of the CRC. It used to be a living room. Now, it housed a couple of computers and an outdated printer. Cynthia hoped she could upgrade the hardware, but it was still usable for now.

'Do you need a hand?' Cynthia asked the woman sitting at the computer by the window. Daisy Jurrah was vigorously shaking the mouse and jolted at Cynthia's voice. 'Sorry. I didn't mean to scare you.'

Daisy shook her head. 'No worries. I was just trying to look something up, but this thing's not working,' she said, holding up the mouse. Cynthia took it and looked for the blinking light.

'Back in a tick.' She returned with a couple of batteries.

'Cheers. Hey, do you reckon you can help me? I want to do a business course so I can help Des with the farm. We want to buy our own soon, so I reckon I should know how to do the books. But I've got no idea where to look.'

Cynthia's eyes lit up, and her chest swelled. 'Absolutely. The CRC has just been approved as a registered training provider.' Daisy gave her a blank stare. 'It means we can run courses like that here.'

Daisy's face transformed as she grinned. 'Deadly. I reckon Des might want to do something too. And my son, Maali, could do with some more schooling.' Cynthia couldn't wipe the smile off her face. Her plan was coming together. She gave Daisy some flyers to pass around, and when she'd left, Cynthia went back to her office. Now that she officially had students, her next step was to apply for a grant to upgrade the computer hardware in the training room. She turned her computer back on and spent the next few hours searching for grants and working on applications. By the time she thought to look at the clock, it was half-past five. She'd made good progress. At least one area of her life was on track.

She pulled up near the cottage to find Tom standing near his ute. Something about his demeanour was off. Cynthia felt a knot form in the pit of her stomach. She approached him and called out. He looked up at her with a blank stare, which he quickly replaced with a forced smile.

'What are you doing out here, hun?' Cynthia asked.

Tom looked around and then back at her. 'Nothing. Just admiring the view,' he said, before pulling her into an embrace and nuzzling her neck. She gently pushed him back and waited until he was looking directly at her.

'I'm making you a doctor's appointment, and that's final. You hear me, Thomas Brody?' He nodded once. Cynthia linked her arm in his, and they walked inside. A car horn beeped, and they turned to see Vitto, the Italian traveller-cum-roustabout Tom had recently hired, pull up in the driveway. He had a fully equipped campervan and ventured out exploring the area whenever he could. Cynthia was used to the backpackers coming and going. She hoped this one would stick around for a while.

'I've refilled the water troughs and feedlots in the back paddocks. I thought I'd head out and explore for a bit,' Vitto said.

'No worries. The ridge has some good views, and there's a waterhole about thirty k's that way,' Tom said, thumb pointing to the right. Cynthia felt relief flood through her. Whatever was going on with Tom, he was still as friendly and helpful as he had always been. Vitto waved as he headed down the driveway. With Vitto helping while Will adjusted to his new life, Tom could focus on himself for once.

Two weeks later, Tom leaned over the kitchen sink in the CRC kitchen so the crumbs from his biscuit wouldn't get on the floor. The man had many endearing qualities, Cynthia thought as she popped the last of her biscuit into her mouth and went back into her office.

'I'll be ready in a sec. I just need to print these flyers,' she called out. Opening her inbox, her eyes flicked through the subject lines, stopping short at an email from the shire. She opened it and scanned the contents, then let out a whoop and pumped the air.

'What's going on?' Tom asked from the doorway.

Cynthia beamed up at him. 'The Shire has approved my grant application. I can get some new computer equipment. This'll help me bring in some new students.'

'That's great, sweetheart.' His words were heartfelt, but Tom's wringing hands betrayed his true feelings.

'Are you ready for your appointment?'

'As much as I can be.'

'Positive thoughts, hun,' Cynthia said, grabbing her handbag.

The waiting room was empty when they arrived. Tom picked up an old copy of Farm Weekly while Cynthia opened her latest book club pick about forbidden love between a farmer's daughter and an Italian POW. Minutes later, Doctor Sunareen led them into his office. Tom sat with his arms folded. Doctor Sunareen looked expectantly from him to Cynthia.

'Tom's been having a few issues with his memory lately,' Cynthia offered.

'I've just been a bit forgetful, that's all.'

'I see,' Doctor Sunareen said, then turned to the computer and scanned his notes. 'You have a family history of dementia.' Tom nodded. 'It might not be that, but it is something we'll need to check.'

Tom, with a little prompting, answered questions about his medical history. As the doctor began the tests, Tom's eyes kept wandering over to Cynthia's face. She sat with a gentle smile playing on her lips as the doctor assessed Tom's memory, language, problem-solving, and attention skills, along with his balance. Tom sat back with his arms folded and a satisfied look on his face. Cynthia hadn't noticed anything out of the ordinary while he'd been performing the tests, but she didn't have a medical degree. From the way he glared at her, it was clear that Tom thought everything had gone well.

'I want to take some blood and urine tests to rule out other conditions. And I want you to have a CT scan and potentially an MRI as well,' Doctor Sunareen said. Tom's face fell. 'We need to check every possibility.'

'So, it might not be dementia then?' Tom asked.

Doctor Sunareen cleared his throat. 'It's too early to say for sure. But there are strong indicators that it may be the case.' Cynthia's body felt heavy. She looked across at Tom. He was staring at the floor, shoulders slumped. She couldn't begin to imagine what was going through his mind. She was already considering the possibilities. They walked back to the CRC in silence. When they were safely hidden away in Cynthia's office, Tom let out a huff. His body shook for a few moments before he took a deep breath.

'Just when things were going well, except for Will's accident, of course. I mean, Kit's having a baby, and I've found you again. Life was good,' he said, shaking his head.

'Life is good. We'll get through this the same way we get through everything else. We take each day as it comes.' She pulled him into a hug, and they stayed in that position for a few moments before Tom leaned back.

'I don't want Kit to know. At least not yet. Actually, I don't want anyone to know.'

'It hasn't even been confirmed yet.'

'I know, but it will. I can feel it. Promise me you won't tell anyone.'

Cynthia heaved a sigh. It was a promise she wished she didn't have to make, but her gut instinct was telling her he was right—the diagnosis would be dementia.

'We'll have to tell people at some point. Especially Kit, she has a right to know.'

'I'm just not ready, and I don't know when I will be.' His voice dipped lower. 'I remember the look that came over people when Dad told them. I don't want to see that look on Kit's face or anyone else's, for that matter.' Cynthia's chest tightened. She couldn't imagine how Tom must feel knowing that he could suffer the same fate as his father. All she could do was be there for him, and she intended to do just that. No matter what.

✪

One pill was useless; two barely scraped the surface of his pain. Will downed three pills and checked the bottle. One day's supply left. Examining the prescription on the kitchen bench, a wave of relief washed over him. He still had one repeat left. Maybe by then the pain would have relinquished its grip on him. Maybe by then he'd feel like himself again. He shoved the script into his pocket and drove into town. It had taken him a few days to get used to driving with one hand. Luckily, he had an automatic, but even so, driving probably wasn't the best idea.

He took the bend and flew past the sign announcing the entrance to Sanderson Ridge. A lump formed in his throat, and his stomach clenched. He'd been so focused on getting his medication that he hadn't thought about what might await him. In a town like this, it was unlikely he could get his script without seeing someone he knew. If he did, what would they say? What would he say?

He braced himself for scrutiny as he pulled up outside the doctor's surgery, which also housed the pharmacy. Will breathed a sigh of relief as he glanced around the empty shop. He pushed the script across the counter towards the pharmacist on duty, who read it and told him it would be about ten minutes. Will sat in a chair, watching the clock on the wall. He'd forgotten his phone, so the wait felt like an eternity. A stocky man decked out in R M Williams gear sidled to the counter, slapped his script down and turned around to take a seat. He stopped short when he saw Will.

'Haven't seen you in town for a while. I heard about the accident. How's it going?' Richard Kellerman asked. The businessman turned town councillor flicked his eyes at Will's arm. Will turned slightly, almost protectively, to the right.

'I'm okay. There's not much I can do about it.'

'I guess not,' Richard said. An awkward silence followed. Will kept his eyes glued to the clock. The pharmacist had said ten minutes, and it had been eight.

'How's Kit? The baby must be due soon,' Richard said.

Will's eyes darted back to Richard's face. 'Still a few more weeks to go.'

Richard nodded and was about to say something when the pharmacist called Will's name. He stood quickly and grabbed the proffered bag before nodding at Richard and striding towards the exit. He rushed out the door and straight into the path of Nate and Kane.

'Will!' they chorused, beaming. Will returned the smile quickly. Nate had visited the farm a few times since the day he'd apologised, but things had continued to be tense between them.

'Let's get a beer, hey,' Kane said, licking his lips. It was almost noon. The pub would fill up during the lunchtime rush. It had been hard enough to see Richard. He certainly wasn't up for facing anyone else who might be in town. Will shook his head.

'Nah, I'd better be getting back. Maybe another time,' he said.

'Come on. Just one pint,' Nate said.

'Not today,' Will said, then waved and rushed past them. He knew they'd be wondering what had gotten into him. He'd never refused a beer before, but things were different now. He was different. Would he ever feel normal again? Would he ever be happy again? He drove back to the farm with music blasting from the speakers. If he turned the music up loud enough, it drained the thoughts spiralling in his head.

✪

Bending down, Kit held the fence railing with one hand and pushed the bottle through with the other. The small pen held four brown and white calves who were still slightly wobbly on their feet. Kit cooed to the closest one and held the bottle so it could suckle, lifting her other hand to pat the soft hair on its head. Its big brown eyes stared back at her, and she wondered where this calf might end up. That was the most challenging aspect of farming, and it was something she tried to avoid thinking about when she could. Lately, her thoughts had turned to the macabre more often. When the bottle was empty, she stood up and put a hand on her lower back. Bending was becoming difficult. She looked past her belly to her toes. She'd probably painted those for the last time, at least for the next few months anyway. They would look dreadful when they chipped, but she wouldn't be able to see them. And from Will's demeanour lately, it seemed that he wouldn't care either.

'That's a big sigh,' a voice said. She gazed upward, recognising the man her father had hired weeks ago. Vitto was a backpacker who was spending his working holiday on farms. Kit had been so caught up with moving into the homestead and dealing with Will's moods that she hadn't spent a lot of time with him. He jumped the fence and tipped a bucket of feed into the trough for the older calves. Kit envied his ability to move unencumbered.

'How was your day off?' she asked, keeping her tone light. Vitto was a nice guy, but he was virtually a stranger. She couldn't vent to him.

'I drove around to the gorge. It's a beautiful spot.'

'Yeah. It is. You should head up to Larranka Pool next time. It's gorgeous at sunset. I'm sure Dad'll let you have more time off if you ask.' She wasn't entirely certain her suggestion would be met with approval by her father, but they had to ensure Vitto stayed around. Will hadn't even hinted that he was ready to start work again. His arm and shoulder seemed to be perpetually sore, and the painkillers that he'd been taking didn't appear to be doing anything to help him.

'I still can't believe how big Australia is. I've been travelling for just over a year, and I feel like I've only seen a small part of it,' Vitto said.

'Ah, there you are,' Tom called out, looking from Kit to Vitto. 'I need a hand tagging some of the newer stock. Would you grab the tags for me?' he said, pointing to the shed. Tom hung back as Vitto walked off.

'How's things, love?' he asked Kit, worry forming in the lines around his eyes.

'All good, Dad.' He tilted his head and waited. Kit was thankful that she'd always had a good relationship with him, except for her wild phase when she was a teenager.

'Well, if I'm honest. Will's still being distant.' She wanted to tell her dad what was going on, but she also didn't want to betray Will. She felt torn.

'He'll come around.'

'Are you sure about that? I feel like he's ignoring me. It's like he's a different person.'

'He is, love. But I don't think his feelings for you have changed.' Kit smiled. She wasn't so sure about that. She wasn't sure about anything anymore. Before the accident, she would have sworn that she'd stand by Will. She did swear she would, in fact, when they married. But now, she was wondering if she could really handle the 'in sickness and in health' part of her vows. She shook the thought from her head and looked up at Tom.

'We might need to get him back to work sooner rather than later. I don't think Vitto will stick around long. He wants to see the country.'

'I think you're right. Leave it with me,' Tom said. Kit spent the rest of the day ticking off her list of tasks. Her body did the work autonomously, but her mind was lost in rumination.

She was famished by the time she walked up to the back verandah of the homestead. The bass hit her first, then the drums, guitar riffs, and screaming vocals. She walked into the living room to find Will sprawled on the couch, chugging back a beer. At least he's not passed out, Kit thought. She moved to his side, and he gulped loudly, eyes wide.

'I didn't hear you come in,' he said.

'That's not surprising,' she said, turning down the volume. She wanted to ask how his day was, but worried it would set him off. She'd been walking on eggshells lately. Instead, she bent to grab the full wash basket that she'd put on the coffee table before heading out that morning. She winced as she stood up and dropped the basket. Leaning back, she put both hands on either side of her stomach. The baby was somersaulting from one side of her womb to the other. She could almost grab its foot or hand or elbow, whichever it was, as it stretched her skin even further than she'd ever thought was possible.

'Oh!' she exclaimed, as it moved again.

'What's wrong?' Will said, standing in front of her, eyes wide. She reached out and took both his hands, laying his left hand on her stomach and holding his right hand in place. She watched as his mouth dropped open, then morphed into a broad grin. It was the first time she'd seen him smile since the accident. He let out a low laugh as the baby kicked again.

'That's incredible,' he said, completely awestruck.

'It is. And this little person is going to be here sooner than we think.' His expression shifted. It was as if he were registering the thought for the first time. His mouth turned down in a frown. 'What's wrong?' she asked.

'I don't know if I can do it,' he said.

Kit froze, her mind racing. 'Do what?'

'Be a good dad. With this,' he said, shifting his head toward his flaccid arm.

'Of course you can,' she said, attempting to stamp down the fear that was rising in her with each passing moment.

Will hesitated. 'I don't know...'

An icy dread washed over Kit as she felt something snap inside her. Will had been feeling sorry for himself for long enough. Yes, he'd been injured in the accident, but it could have been so much worse. He could have been a quadriplegic. He could have died, for goodness' sake. And she would have been raising this baby on her own.

'Either you're with me, or you're not. I've had enough of you moping about. I can't do this anymore,' she said, pushing his hands away and rushing to their bedroom. Scrunching her eyes tight, she tried to stop the flow of tears, but it was no use. Her thoughts circled as tears slid down, drenching her pillow. Did she really feel that way? Did she want him gone? Or was it just pregnancy hormones on overdrive? She wasn't sure. What she knew was that she breathed a sigh of relief later that night when she heard him settling in on the couch.

Chapter 5

With a stiff neck and aching back, Will woke up to the sounds of cupboard doors slamming shut, utensils jostling, and the kettle being turned on with no regard for the weakness of the small plastic switch. Clearly, Kit was still in a bad mood. Will thought back to their argument. One minute, they were sharing a moment of new-parent bliss, and the next, she'd delivered him an ultimatum. Things had been strained since the accident, but surely their relationship hadn't degraded to the point of permanent breakage. Fighting the urge to stretch, Will considered his options. He could lie there and pretend to be asleep until she left the house. Or he could face her and potentially have an argument before his meds had kicked in. The decision was made for him when the sliding door slammed.

Breathing a sigh of relief, Will got up, heading straight for the medicine cabinet. The little white pills were the only thing keeping the pain at bay. He checked the bottle. There was about a week's supply left, but he had a doctor's appointment in an hour. He tossed the bottle onto the bench next to some brochures. Kit had a tendency to leave paperwork and pamphlets all over the house, even though she had an office. He stopped short when he realised what they were for. Kit had researched companies that completed car modifications for people with disabilities. That word still annoyed him, but it didn't change the fact that he was now considered disabled or differently-abled, as Kit liked to say. Next to the brochures was an antenatal care pamphlet from the hospital. Will's chest felt as if it had been wrenched open, and his heart pounded in his ears as if being squeezed. How could he have been so selfish? He'd told her he didn't think he could be a dad, as if there was any stopping it, as if she could change it. His fingertips remembered the bump they'd received from inside her stomach. Their baby was coming. And if he wanted to be in its life and Kit's, he had to pull his head in. He had been moping around, feeling sorry for himself, for long enough.

The waiting area was chock-full of coughing kids and sniffling adults. Will groaned inwardly as he sat as far away from the other patients as he could and kept his eyes glued to his phone screen. He almost launched himself into the air when the doctor called his name. Sitting in the office, he jiggled his leg and pulled his lame hand onto his lap, wincing for effect.

'I'm just after another script for the pain meds, please,' Will said. Doctor Sunareen eyed him and then looked at the screen.

'It looks like you've gone through the last script quite quickly. Have you been taking more than the prescribed dose?' he asked.

Will shifted in his seat. 'Yeah. Just when the pain is bad.'

The doctor's mouth set firmly, and his forehead creased with worry lines. 'The pain should be easing at this point, not getting worse. I'll write you one more script, and then we'll have to reassess things. Other than that, how have things been?'

Will contemplated telling him about his fears of what fatherhood might bring and whether he could handle it. He fiddled with his wedding ring. No, he had to focus on the positives. Perhaps if the doctor could see he was trying, then he'd be lenient with him the next time Will asked for a prescription.

'I'm thinking of getting mods for the car and going back to work, just light duties of course.'

Doctor Sunareen nodded. 'Excellent idea. You're lucky you live out here in the country. I dare say you wouldn't have been able to drive in the city one-handed. Not to mention the legality of the situation. Let me know once it's done, and I'll sign a clearance just in case you do run into any trouble.'

With the new prescription in hand, Will drove back to the farm, ruminating as the bass thumped through the speakers. He could make this his last prescription, but the doctor thought he was on the mend, so it shouldn't be an issue to get another. He would contact the mob to get the modifications done on his car. He'd have to make it up to Kit somehow. And he'd go and see Tom about starting back at work. Probably tomorrow. Or the next day. Depending on how his shoulder felt. His phone rang, and Tom's name flashed on the screen.

'Hey mate. I know it's a big ask, but is there any chance you can help me with the tagging this arvo? Vitto's taken the day off and Kit's at the CRC with Cynthia.' Will's stomach clenched. He had been hoping to ease into it in his own time. But Tom wouldn't ask for help if he didn't need it. Will popped another painkiller as he pulled into the driveway.

Grabbing a bunch of tags off the bench, Will found Tom grunting with the effort of wrangling an unruly calf into the chute. Relief flooded his features when he noticed Will. Ear tagging was a task they'd completed many times before. The difference now was that Will had to figure out how to do his part with only one useful hand. He placed the tags on an upturned bucket next to where they stood, then grabbed the rag to clean the calf's ears. Once it was contained in the chute, the calf sensed it had lost the battle and stood waiting. Will wiped the ear, then shoved a tag into the applicator. He turned to face the calf and hesitated. What if he hit the wrong spot? He looked around, but Tom was already wrestling another calf into position. He took a deep breath, then lined the applicator up and squeezed it firmly. It jolted, and he pulled it away, then checked the tag's placement.

'All good?' Tom asked. Will nodded, then recorded the tag number on the spreadsheet while Tom tagged the next calf in line. They spent the next few hours jostling calves in and out of the chute. It was hard yakka, so when Tom pulled two beers from the fridge, Will was so thirsty the liquid barely hit the sides.

'Thanks for your help. If Kit hadn't told me to give Vitto the day off, then run off with Cynthia, things would have been alright,' Tom said, then took a swig of beer. So Kit had a hand in this? Was it before or after she'd given him the ultimatum?

'No worries. It was good to get back into it,' Will said. He had enjoyed being busy, and he'd forgotten about the pain and his frustrations, at least for a while. Maybe it had been the right time to start back. Maybe if he hadn't been forced, he'd have put it off for much longer. Maybe he should trust Kit with the truth, but would she be able to accept it?

✪

The presenter chimed in as the first of the racers hit the mat. Kit wasn't into reality TV, but this show had her glued to the television every time. She dreamt about being a contestant, travelling to amazing places all over the world, and completing crazy challenges. She'd pictured her and Will having the adventure of a lifetime together. As the couple on screen kissed and gushed about their love for each other, she cringed. She and Will would probably have been like that. Before the accident. Before Will changed. Before she thought she'd had enough. She sprinkled a handful of salt and vinegar chips into the bowl and mixed them into the vanilla ice cream. Her cravings had become stranger as the months ticked by. Some were too weird, but this latest invention was one she might consider keeping after the baby arrived. The saltiness of the chips mixed with the sweetness of the ice cream. It was a party in her mouth. Swallowing a spoonful, she gulped as Will came into the living room, awkwardly pulling a shirt on, his hair still slick from the shower. She couldn't deny that she was attracted to him. Heck, who wouldn't be?

105

'Cool. I'm glad they came first this leg,' Will said, sitting next to her, their thighs touching. He looked at the bowl in her hands and balked. 'What the heck is that?' She feigned nonchalance as she told him the answer. He shook his head and let out a small laugh. They'd barely spoken since their argument, save for the odd 'hi' and 'bye', and here he was acting as if nothing had happened. She stared at him, waiting for some sort of explanation. It took him a few minutes to tear his eyes away from the television screen.

'What?' he asked.

'Um. Are we going to discuss what happened?' Kit asked. He shrugged. 'I need to know where you stand with this, with us.'

'Well, you made it perfectly clear where you stand,' he shot back. Kit felt hot tears sting her eyes. Blinking them back, she threw the bowl onto the coffee table, edged herself off the lounge, and stalked to the bedroom. Why was he being so awful? All she wanted was to know what was going on with him. Was he going to stick around, or was he going to leave her to raise this baby on her own? She hoped to fall into an exhausted sleep, but instead she spent half the night ruminating on their arguments and what it meant for their marriage. She'd thought she could handle whatever this accident threw at them, but what if it was too much?

The doorbell jingled as Kit entered the General Store, which also housed Charlotte's interior design business. Charlotte was almost like a surrogate little sister to Kit. She'd loved watching Charlotte's confidence grow with every completed revamp. After last night's tiff with Will, Kit wanted to focus on something good, and she brimmed with excitement at being able to hire Charlotte for a special project. Kane was serving a customer, so she gave him a quick wave and headed to the corner of the store where Charlotte was sitting at her laptop. She glanced up as Kit approached, her eyebrows shooting up.

'Whoa! You've popped out,' she said with a laugh.

Kit plopped into the chair opposite Charlotte's desk with a grunt. 'I know. I feel like a whale,' she said, puffing out her cheeks.

'Angela said the same thing. Her sickness is gone now.'

'Yeah, mine has too. Besides the fact that I'm lugging this belly around, I'm feeling pretty good at the moment.'

'That's great. So, how can I help?'

Kit couldn't help grinning like a Cheshire cat. She sat forward and placed her hands on the desk, acting businesslike.

'I'd like Lottie Designs to decorate the nursery for my first child.'

Charlotte squealed and ran around the desk to hug Kit. 'OMG! That would be amazing. I have so many ideas already.'

They both turned as the doorbell jingled, and Angela walked in.

'Why do you look so pleased with yourself?' Angela asked Charlotte.

'Kit just asked me to design her nursery.'

'Oh, snap!' Angela said. 'I was just coming in to do that.' The three women burst out laughing, then spent the next hour poring over potential themes and colour schemes, planning to make a start as soon as possible. Kit left feeling lighter. She hadn't realised how much she'd needed to focus on something positive.

The next morning after Will had left the house, Kit headed into her old bedroom. It was like a time machine teleporting her to the late nineties and early noughties. Posters from magazines covered the walls, a deflated blow-up sofa was bundled in one corner, and her six-stacker CD player sat on top of her chest of drawers. She had thought about using the spare bedroom, but it had also doubled as her mum's craft room, and she didn't think her emotional state was ready to tackle those memories. She'd already spent so much time during this pregnancy wishing that her mother were alive so she could ask her all the niggling questions that popped into her head.

Kit pressed play on the CD player, then reached up and pulled an Oasis poster off the wall, shoving it into the waiting garbage bag. As the Teen Hits 2000 CD blasted her into the past, the nesting phase kicked into gear. She bundled up clothes and trinkets for the church charity shop, threw out a bunch of stuff her teen self had thought was precious, and readied the room for renovation. Angela and Charlotte's voices came down the hallway.

'Wow. You've been busy,' Angela said.

'Once I got on a roll, I couldn't stop.'

'Well, you've made my job easier,' Charlotte said as she laid painting sheets over the furniture and floor. 'Now, you two clear out so I can paint.' Kit and Angela grabbed garbage bags and boxes and packed them into the back of Kit's car. By the time they'd stacked the boot and made coffee, Charlotte had already finished the first coat.

'That looks awesome, Lottie. I love the colour,' Kit said.

'Yeah. It'll work for a boy or a girl.'

Kit parked herself on the top step of the stool Lottie had been using and sighed.

'I wish Mum was here for this,' Kit said.

'I know how you feel,' Angela said.

Charlotte took a long sip of coffee, then moved to the window. ' I reckon they are here. Our mums. They're always watching over us.'

Kit smiled. She'd always thought that too, but it was nice to hear someone else say it. 'Plus, you've got an amazing step-mum in Cynthia.'

'That's true,' Kit said as Will stuck his head around the doorway.

'What's going on in here then?' he asked. Kit swallowed the lump in her throat and forced a smile. She hadn't told him she was planning to make this the nursery.

Then again, it wasn't as if they'd spoken much the last week or so. She felt Angela's eyes on her.

'Just getting things ready for the baby. He or she will be here before we know it. We're doing my nursery next,' Angela said. Kit nodded.

'Right. Well, I'll leave you to it,' Will said. His eyes landed on Kit's before he moved down the hallway. Kit felt a hand on her shoulder and looked up into Angela's face.

'All good?' she asked.

'Yeah. You know how it is,' Kit said. She knew Angela would see right through it, but it didn't feel like the right time to get into it. Besides, Will had been trying lately. She just wasn't sure she was ready to accept his efforts.

✪

The bunting swayed in the slight breeze coming in through the open window. Cynthia took a deep breath and puffed her cheeks out as she blew up what felt like the hundredth balloon. The front room of the community resource centre was a sea of pink and blue with some white thrown in for balance. Charlotte and Cynthia had worked together to plan the combined baby shower for Angela and Kit. As Cynthia tied a piece of pink ribbon around another balloon, she looked out the window and saw people walking up the front path.

'The guests are arriving already,' she said, panic rising in her voice. 'We need to get our butts into gear.' Charlotte gave her a thumbs-up, then moved at lightning speed to finish decorating the table and setting up the games. Cynthia hung

110

the last bunch of balloons, smoothed down her hair, and went to the door to greet the arrivals. Everyone oohed and aahed when they entered the room. Streamers ran from each corner of the ceiling to the balloon centrepiece, hanging in the middle. The white tablecloths were covered with vases holding bunches of pink and blue, fake but altogether lifelike gerberas. A table had been set up on the side for the presents, and another was filled with nappies, chocolate bars, tape measures, and other items they'd use later during the games. Cynthia stood at the doorway, buzzing with excitement and pride.

The door swung open, and the guests of honour walked in. Both stopped short at the entrance, mouths agape, eyes wide.

'Welcome to your baby shower!' Cynthia said. Everyone cheered as Angela and Kit's looks of surprise turned into joy.

'This is amazing,' Kit exclaimed.

'Yeah. It looks incredible,' Angela said.

'That was all your sister's doing,' Cynthia said.

'You had a big hand in this, too,' Charlotte said. Cynthia put a hand up in surrender, but inside, she was thrilled to know that the girls were pleased. It was about them, after all. While the guests mingled, Cynthia went back and forth from the kitchen, bringing in the food and drinks and setting them up on the table in the middle of the room. Charlotte was already organising the games. Time flew by as the guests played guess the baby food, blindfolded nappy change, and predicted the baby's stats. Nate caused a controversy when he refused to do the blindfolded nappy change. He was ribbed by every other male in the room, except Will.

Cynthia waited for a lull in the conversation, then announced that it was time to open presents. Angela and Kit sat at the far end of the room while the guests mingled around them. Charlotte and Cynthia each grabbed a gift, and everyone watched on as the two soon-to-be mums opened them one by one. Cynthia handed her gifts to both women. Her eyes glistened as Kit read aloud the inscription she'd written.

'Have courage and dust off your wings; let the beauty of your next journey begin to unfold.' Kit wiped her palms across her eyes, then reached up to hug Cynthia. 'Thank you. That's lovely.'

'I'm so glad I can be with you on this part of your journey,' Cynthia whispered into her ear. She guessed that the feeling she felt at that moment was exactly what a proud soon-to-be-grandmother would feel. Kit may not be her own flesh and blood, but Cynthia had grown to love her fiercely.

With the party drawing to a close, Cynthia cleared up the food and drinks. Removing the decorations could wait until the next day. She heard the back door open and heavy footsteps tread down the hallway. She knew who it was before he materialised in the doorway.

'How did it go?' Tom asked.

'It was great. I think Ang and Kit enjoyed themselves. That's the main thing,' Cynthia said as she pecked him on the cheek. 'You could have stuck around, you know. There were other men here.'

Tom shrugged a shoulder. 'Nah. It's not really my thing,' he said. 'You ready to go?' Cynthia nodded, then went into her office to grab her handbag before following Tom out to the car. He opened the door for her, then went around to the driver's side. Cynthia buckled up and then waited for him to start the engine. He took his time, and Cynthia had to bite her tongue. Tom had his ways, and she wasn't going to change them by nagging him. When they reached the end of the CRC driveway, the car sat idle. Cynthia looked across at Tom, and her heart froze. A deep furrow creased his brow, and his lips were compressed into an unwavering line. She waited a moment, then put a hand on his leg.

'Tom? What's wrong?'

He looked at her, and his lip trembled. He shook his head and gripped the steering wheel until his knuckles turned white.

'I can't...I don't know which way to go,' he whispered, his eyes downcast. Cynthia's breath quickened, and a knot formed in her stomach. When the doctor had finally confirmed Tom's diagnosis, he warned them about what was to come—disorientation, confusion, memory loss, trouble planning and problem-solving. They'd sat stony-faced, listening. Both assumed that those things were in the distant future. This is it, Cynthia thought. This is the start. She'd read enough webpages and books by now to know that it was best not to make him feel bad about it.

'Well, you always take the lead. I think it's about time I took a turn driving us home. What do you say?' she said, trying to keep her voice light. Tom nodded and hopped out without looking at her. She walked around the back of the car.

'Everything alright?' Rose was standing on the footpath outside the CRC, watching them. Cynthia suppressed a groan. Rose was the one person in town that Cynthia did not want to deal with during one of Tom's episodes. She plastered a smile on her face.

'We're fine. I just felt like driving.' She waved at Rose as she turned down the main street and headed towards the farm. Her head was spinning. What if Tom couldn't drive from now on? What if he drove and ended up getting lost? What if this is the beginning of the end? And what if Rose suspects something's going on? She'll be on the case like a detective in a murder mystery.

Tom broke the silence. 'I meant what I said. I don't want anyone to know, especially Kit.' They'd had disagreements about his stance since the initial visit to Doctor Sunareen. Cynthia thought Kit had a right to know, but she understood his hesitation. But would finding out that your father had dementia be easier before or after having a baby? Cynthia wasn't sure.

Chapter 6

Kit tried to ignore the dull ache in her stomach as she stacked the freshly washed baby clothes into the drawers in the newly completed nursery. The pains had been happening on and off for weeks, but Doctor Sunareen had assured her it was just Braxton Hicks. As the day wore on, the discomfort intensified, eventually compelling Kit to ask Will for a heat pack. The pains had settled down as evening approached, and Kit had managed to lay the sheets and rugs on the cot in the nursery along with the bassinet that would stay by the bed in the master bedroom. Now the sensation was back with a vengeance. It felt as if something was building up inside her. She stood up and put a hand on her stomach. It was as hard as a basketball. She tried to recall the last time she'd felt the baby move, and when she couldn't, a sense of panic rose in her. Was the baby alright? How was she supposed to feel it in her rock-hard stomach? Will glanced into the nursery as he walked down the hallway and stopped mid-stride.

'What's wrong? Is it the baby?' he asked, his voice rising at the end of the sentence.

'I don't know. It's probably nothing.'

'It doesn't look like nothing. I'm taking you to the hospital.' Will dashed towards the bedroom and emerged with her pre-packed hospital bag hanging from his shoulder.

'I think it's too ear—.' Kit winced as a strong contraction took her breath away.

'I don't think so. Let's go,' Will said, grabbing the keys. She stood in the nursery, unable to move. If she moved from this spot, then it was really happening. She was really going to have to push this baby out. She was really going to be a mum.

'Kit? Come on. It's alright,' Will said, cradling her arm in his good one. He looked across at her several times on the way to the car, then opened the door and helped her ease herself into the passenger seat. The modifications had been completed on his ute only two weeks prior. Kit watched him walk to the driver's side; his eyes were wide, but a grin spread across his face. The drive to the hospital seemed to take an eternity as the pain tugged at Kit's midsection, but Will was driving over the speed limit. They called Tom and Cynthia to let them know what was happening. Tom seemed to be in shock, but Cynthia took over the conversation, wishing them the best of luck. They made it to the hospital in record time, and Kit sat waiting while Will went inside to see the nurse on duty. She closed her eyes as another contraction hit. They were down to five minutes apart. Kit took a deep breath. Was this really happening? Was she about to have a baby? Was it going to hurt? Would he or she be alright? The car door opened, and Will stood next to Samantha. Kit sat back, head lifted. Of all the people to be on duty, it had to be Samantha. She and her clique had bullied Kit during high school. They'd been civil with each other since entering adulthood, but Kit would never forget what Samantha and her friend Jamie were like. From what Will was saying, she was the only one on duty. There was nothing for it. Samantha was going to be the one to help her become a mum. Kit eased herself out of the seat and into the waiting wheelchair. It felt over the top, but apparently, it was protocol. Before they entered the building, Kit took one last look up at the starry sky. Wish me luck, Mum, she thought.

Will stood next to the bed, his fingers gently squeezing Kit's hand. Samantha had settled her into one of the private rooms and gone to call Doctor Sunareen. Kit's stomach still felt hard, and the contractions were still five minutes apart. She looked up at Will.

'Are we ready for this?' she asked.

'There's no stopping it now,' Will said, chuckling. It was alright for him. He wasn't the one who was about to be in intense pain for who knew how long. Kit squeezed her eyes shut as another contraction hit. She heard someone come into the room.

'Doctor Sunareen is about ten minutes away. Do you mind if I check your progress?' Samantha asked. Kit shot a look at Will, then nodded. After an uncomfortable examination, Samantha resurfaced with a smile. 'You're eight centimetres dilated. This baby will be on its way soon.' Will squeezed her hand, but all she could do was stare at the wall in front of her as fear gripped her.

'I don't think I can do this,' she said.

'Of course you can,' Samantha said. She laid a cool cloth across Kit's forehead as another contraction came on. Kit felt helpless and nervous. Minutes later, Doctor Sunareen entered the room and took over with an air of authority that relaxed Kit's nervousness. He checked her dilation and was pleased to report that she'd reached the magic ten centimetres, which meant she was fully effaced. He pushed on her stomach, checking the baby's position, before checking Kit's blood pressure and heart rate.

'Try to rest in between the contractions. You're going to need all your strength,' Doctor Sunareen said. It was easy for him to say. Kit tried to rest, but the contractions felt like they were only seconds apart. The passage of time seemed like an anomaly. She had no idea how long they'd been at the hospital for or how long it had been since her last contraction. Everything merged as her body prepared.

'Are you sure you don't want something for the pain?' Will asked her. She shook her head and puffed the air out of her cheeks.

'It's a bit late for that now,' Doctor Sunareen said, his head poking up from the sheet that had been placed across Kit's lower half. Following the doctor's orders, she pushed and puffed with each contraction.

'Ouch!' Will squeaked when she squeezed his hand.

'Really? I'm pushing a baby out of me. Toughen up,' she moaned. With a final push, she felt an enormous sense of relief flood her body as the baby was born, and a piercing cry filled the room. Will cut the umbilical cord, and Doctor Sunareen handed the baby to Samantha, who wiped it clean, then wrapped it and placed it on Kit's chest.

'Well, is it a boy or a girl?' Will asked.

Doctor Sunareen smiled. 'Congratulations! You have a baby boy,' he said. Will let out a whoop, and Kit laughed as she stared at her baby's face, mesmerised. This baby was the most beautiful baby she had ever seen, and she was struck by an overwhelming, all-encompassing love for him. She knew in that instant that she would do anything for him. He was her world.

'Do you have a name for him?' Samantha asked as she took photos with Kit's camera. Will placed a hand on the baby's head and smiled down at the mother and baby.

'His name is Elijah Joseph Stone,' Will said, then leaned down and planted a kiss on the baby's head, then one on Kit's lips. 'You did it, Kit. I'm so proud of you,' he whispered.

After Samantha and Doctor Sunareen assisted Kit in birthing the placenta, they left the room so the new family could be alone. Kit continued to stare at her baby. Will wrapped his arm around them both. It was as if they were the only people on the planet. She unwrapped the baby and checked over his entire body. Everything was where it should be. Ten fingers and ten toes. A cute button nose. And the softest hair she'd ever touched.

Will took a deep breath and turned to face Kit.

'Sorry for being a tosser,' he said. 'I want you to know that I'm all in. I'm going to get myself together. I'll make it work, this stupid arm be damned.' Kit's lip quivered. 'Don't cry, or you'll make me cry.' He would too. He was a total softie. Kit smiled up at him. Maybe it was the endorphins running through her, or just the fact that she loved him, but nothing else mattered. They were a family.

'We'll make this work. We have to,' she said. He leaned forward and kissed her gently.

The room filled with Cynthia's voice after a loud knock echoed through the space.

'Can we come in? We're dying to see our grandchild,' Cynthia said. Will called out for her and Tom to come in. Cynthia rushed over to the bed and hugged Kit before gushing over the newborn. Tom kissed Kit on the forehead, then shook Will's hand.

'What a ripper,' he said. 'He's going to be an excellent farmer. I can tell.'

Kit's eyes sparkled as a wide beam spread across her face. 'He's got an awesome grandad to teach him,' she said. A warmth bloomed in her chest, a feeling so potent she could almost physically feel it expand. A soft sniffle broke the silence, and her gaze met Tom's. A single tear traced a glistening path down his cheek.

Will sat in the car, rubbing fatigue from his eyes and waking his senses. He'd tossed and turned all night, desperate for morning to arrive so he could return to the hospital to see Kit and Elijah. The general store was open, and Kane and Charlotte were behind the counter, laughing at an in-joke. Will stood in front of the flower display, chewing the inside of his cheek. Would gerberas be alright, or would Kit want roses?

'Need a hand?' Charlotte asked.

'Yeah. What do you get a woman who's just given birth?' Will replied with a cheeky grin. Charlotte let out a squeal and pulled him into a hug.

'OMG! Did Kit have the baby? Was it a boy or a girl?' Charlotte asked. Kane came over and shook his hand, patting his back with the other.

'A boy. We've named him Elijah Joseph.'

'Oh, that's sweet. When can we see her?' Charlotte said.

'Not sure. Maybe later today. I'll get her to text you. Now, which flowers should I get?' Charlotte worked her magic and created a gorgeous bunch of flowers.

'No charge,' she responded when Will attempted to pay. On a high from sharing the news, Will went across the road to Beth's, grabbed two coffees and smiled graciously as Beth showered him with congratulations. He drove to the hospital and checked himself in the rear-view mirror. There were dark bags under his tired eyes. He took a sip of his coffee, the bitter taste helping to wake him even more, and then ventured inside.

Kit was propped up with pillows, breastfeeding Elijah. Her serene face was illuminated by the gentle morning light coming through the window. Will had never been more enamoured with her than he was in that moment. He dropped the flowers on the end of the bed, then kissed her on the forehead and handed her a coffee. She raised her eyebrows.

'It's decaf. Beth says congrats. So do Lottie and Kane,' Will said, taking a seat on the chair by the bed. Kit let out a satisfied sigh as she took a sip. They both laughed as the baby let out a grunt.

'You're a natural,' Will said, indicating the now sleeping baby.

'I don't know about that. Samantha had to give me some pointers sometime around midnight when he wouldn't latch on properly.' She looked down at the baby nestled peacefully in her arms. 'Isn't he the most gorgeous thing you've ever seen?' Will agreed. 'Do you want to hold him? You didn't do it last night.' Will froze, stomach tensed. He wanted to hold his son more than anything, but what if he somehow hurt him? As if sensing his trepidation, Kit added, 'You won't drop him.' Kit moved slowly, swinging her legs over the side of the bed, wincing as she stood up. Will sat bolt upright. Kit laid Elijah in the crook of his left arm and placed his right arm over the top of the warm bundle. Will's eyes did not leave Elijah's face as Kit took photos. He felt a tear at the corner of his eye and tried to blink it away. Kit leaned down and kissed him, then stood back. Will grinned, his eyes lighting up as she snapped more photos.

'See. What did it tell you?' Kit said. 'Can you hold him while I have a shower?' When he heard the water running, he looked down at the baby, who was now looking around the room, eyes blinking slowly.

'Hey, buddy. Hey Elijah. I'm your dad. I want you to know that I'm going to try to be the best dad I can, even with this dodgy arm.' A gurgle escaped Elijah, and in that moment, Will's heart was overflowing with affection for this tiny human that he had helped to create.

Driving home from the hospital a day later, as a family of three, was the most surreal feeling. They were officially parents, and they were in charge of keeping this little defenceless human alive for the next eighteen years. Will's body tingled with the sharp, electric feeling of nerves. Kit rested a hand on his leg, and he felt himself relax. Tom and Cynthia waved from the cottage as they drove past them towards the homestead. Kit didn't wait for him to open her door. She was out of the car with her head in the back, unlocking the buckles, before Will had walked around from the driver's side. He shuffled her bag onto his good shoulder and followed them inside. Elijah was asleep, so Kit headed straight to the nursery. Will watched from the doorway as she gently placed him in his cot. He looked around the room.

Charlotte had done an amazing job decorating it. Although now that they knew the baby was a boy, they could add some more masculine touches to it. They stood above the cot, hand in hand, peering down at their prodigy. Will hoped with every fibre of his being that he could keep his promise.

The alarm buzzed Will out of his dream. He reached across to stop it before it woke Kit up. He needn't have worried. She was already up, sitting in the rocking chair, feeding Elijah. Will lay his arm behind his head and watched her for a moment. Dressed in a white nightie, with her dark hair flowing down past her shoulders, she looked like a goddess.

'You were pushing out some zzzs,' Kit teased.

'Yeah. It's a tough life being a dad,' he joked. Kit poked her tongue out at him, and he wished he could take her then and there. But now there was another person in the room to consider. It had been two weeks since Elijah was born. As if on cue, he unlatched and gurgled. Kit sat him up on her knees with her hand under his chin, gently patting his back. He decided that was the time to power spew all over her. Kit groaned, and Will laughed.

'Oh ha ha,' she said, standing and moving towards the bed. 'Here. You take him while I clean this up.' She placed Elijah on Will's chest, and he put his hand on the baby's back. The next thing he heard was a splatter from the baby's nappy region, followed by a smell that rivalled what the farm animals let out.

'Ew, gross, Eli. That's rotten,' he said, then tried to sit up. It was almost impossible for him to push himself up while Elijah was lying on his chest. He tried to roll him towards the bed, but stopped. What if he hurt him? He used his good arm to pull his limp arm across Elijah's back, steadying him as best he could so that he could at least sit up. Gently and slowly, he wriggled his way into a sitting position, then used his working arm to move Elijah onto the bed. He got up and grabbed a nappy and a clean onesie, then stood above the baby. How was he supposed to change Elijah with one hand? It was impossible. Frustration boiled inside him, and he threw the nappy and clothes down on the bed just as Kit came out of the bathroom.

'What's up?' she asked.

'I'm late for work,' he said, ignoring her questioning look as he changed and marched towards the door. He stopped in the kitchen and downed two pills, hoping they would dull his thoughts as well as the pain.

✪

Cynthia and Tom sat on the verandah enjoying a coffee and a slice of the homemade lemon and ginger cake Cynthia had baked earlier that morning. Sundays were her favourite day of the week. Some days, they attended the morning service at the little church in town that Tom had been going to for years. On other days, they took things a little slower, sleeping in longer, and only doing the necessary jobs around the farm before relaxing at home. She took a sip of coffee and chuckled as Tom let out a moan after his first bite of cake.

'That good, is it?'

'Bloody oath. I love your cooking, sweetheart.' A wave of warmth washed over Cynthia's body. She'd never tire of hearing compliments from Tom. Her phone rang, and she ran inside to answer it, returning a few minutes later with a grin.

'That was Nate. Angela has had a baby boy. They've named him Ethan Jack,' Cynthia said. She looked at Tom, expecting an exclamation of happiness, but a shadow of sadness crossed his face. 'What's wrong? Are you alright?' Was he having an episode? He brushed away her concern with his next remark.

'I'm fine. Jack was Angela's dad's name.'

'Oh, I see. Well, that's a lovely tribute to him,' Cynthia said, taking a bite of cake.

'Yeah. It is. Do you think Kit will name her next son after me? After I'm gone,' Tom said.

The cake felt like sandpaper in Cynthia's throat, causing her to cough violently. 'I sure hope you'll be around a lot longer than that. You'll be here long enough to teach Elijah, and any other children they have, how to work this farm.'

'I wish I had your optimism,' Tom said, looking across the paddocks. He waved at Vitto as he made his way over to the verandah. Vitto's shoulders sagged, and he dragged his feet, the gravel crunching under his shoes. He stood in front of them and took off his hat. Cynthia's stomach churned.

'Tom. Cynthia. I...uh...I want to thank you for giving me this job, but I think it's time I moved on. I'm officially handing in my notice. I'll be off on Saturday,' he said, looking at the ground. The timing couldn't have been worse. Kit had only had Elijah two weeks prior; Will was only just taking on farm work again, and Tom's illness was progressing faster than they'd realised it would.

'I'm sorry to do this. I know you have a lot going on. But my visa only has a few months left, and there's still so much I want to see,' Vitto said. Tom still hadn't moved. No doubt trying to figure out how he was going to get everything done now that he would be a man down.

Cynthia gave Vitto a sympathetic smile. 'We understand. You've got to do what you've got to do. We'll work something out,' she said, then gently kicked Tom's foot. He sprang to life as if he were a wind-up toy.

'Yeah. All good, mate. Thanks for your help. I'll get you squared away with pay, and you can see the rest of our beautiful country.'

'Thank you. Grazie. I appreciate it,' Vitto said, relief flooding off him like heatwaves. He nodded at them both, then turned and made his way back to the shed where he'd parked his camper. Tom sighed deeply and put his head back on the chair. Cynthia finished her coffee while she waited. She knew Tom had to process this latest development before he'd talk to her about it. She didn't have to wait long. He turned to her and shook his head.

'Well, it's shocking timing, but there's not much we can do about it. I might head to the pub later and see if I can rouse up someone else to help.' Cynthia's mind flew back to the afternoon of Kit and Angela's baby shower. Tom guessed her thoughts. 'If anything happens, I'll call you.' She stood up and sat on his lap, wrapping her arms around his neck.

'You'd better, Mr Brady,' she said, planting a kiss on his lips.

Chapter 7

Will used his feet to keep the fence pole in place and rubbed his shoulder. The dull ache had infiltrated his day. He'd popped some painkillers when he was out of Tom's sight, but it had been a few hours since his last dose. Vitto had left the farm the week before, and Tom hadn't had any luck finding a replacement, so he'd had to quickly find ways to complete the tasks. Every morning, he'd wake up with an ache and an urge to take painkillers, and he'd take them repeatedly as the day wore on. At night, he'd swallow a couple right before bed so that he could get through until morning. The only problem was that the bottle was emptying quickly, and he hadn't been back to face Doctor Sunareen since his last, almost unsuccessful visit. He held the pole upright while Tom filled in around it with dirt, then Will stamped it down while Tom wiped the sweat from his brow.

'Looks like your shoulder's giving you the jip. I reckon we should call it a day, hey?' Tom said. They packed up their tools and walked towards the ute. Will looked back at the spot where they'd been mending the fence.

'You forgetting something?' he said, looking across at Tom. The older man glanced around, then spotted his tool bag on the ground.

'Geez. I'd forget my head if it wasn't screwed on,' he joked. Will climbed into the cab while Tom lifted the tool bag onto the tray. 'Did I tell you this bag belonged to my dad? He was born right here on this farm and worked it his entire life.' Will froze for a moment. He'd heard this story before. Would it be impolite to tell Tom? He kept quiet. The sooner he got home, the sooner he could take some more painkillers.

'Really? That's pretty cool,' he said. Tom grinned and started the engine as Will's phone beeped with a text.

Head wetting at the pub tonight? We've gotta celebrate our boys. Nate's message was brief. It was an olive branch. Will looked out the window. Was he ready to accept it?

Hell yeah, I'm in. Will shot back. Pain be damned. He hadn't had a night out in ages, and what better reason was there than to celebrate the birth of their sons? He asked Tom if he wanted to join them, but he shook his head.

'Nah, I'm not feeling up to it. But if you can rustle up a farmhand for me, that'd be good,' he said. When they reached the homestead, Will said goodbye and headed inside. Kit was already cooking dinner, carrying Elijah in a sling in front of her.

'I won't be home for dinner. Nate and I are going to the pub,' he said. He paused at the doorway, unsure whether or not he should kiss her. Things had been dicey between them again. He'd thought Kit's mood swings would end when her pregnancy did, but that hadn't been the case. 'I'll just have a quick shower before I go.' By the time he got out, Kit was in the nursery. Elijah was whimpering, but he'd soon settle. Then Kit would have the house to herself. Surely she'd be happy about that. Will was out the door and in the ute, popping another pill and putting the ute into drive, before she got the chance to ask him to stay.

The bar and restaurant were full. They usually were on a Saturday night. Half of the footy team was there, and some of the local farmers. He bought a round of drinks and wished Kit still worked there. The discount made the prices more palatable. It was good to be out, though. He handed a beer to Nate, then grabbed his own, standing with his lame arm closest to the bar.

'Cheers to our boys, Ethan and Elijah. May they grow up to be best mates,' Nate said, glass in the air.

'Here, here,' Will added, before the group took long gulps. He let out a sigh of appreciation. 'Geez, I needed this. I feel like I haven't been out in ages.'

'You've had a lot going on,' Dave, the footy player and ambulance officer, said with a shrug.

'Yeah. We've been keeping the bar up for you,' Kane said, chuckling.

'Well, here's to a long night ahead,' Will said, then finished his beer. Nate bought the next round. Everyone was keen to congratulate them on becoming first-time dads. The older lads were full of advice. 'Happy wife, happy life' seemed to be a favourite platitude. 'Yes, dear' was another one. Will smiled and nodded. He'd parent his own way, but it was only polite to listen when advice was given.

Round after round, Will kept up the pace. He soon swayed his way into the men's room. Standing in front of the mirror, he smoothed down his shirt. His fingers stopped on the bulge of the two pills he'd shoved in his pocket before he'd left the house. He looked at his reflection, eyes darting to the arm hanging on his right side. He willed it to move, but of course it didn't. It never would again. He let out a snort and downed the pills in one gulp. Back in the bar, Shirley was calling for last drinks as *Closing Time* by Semisonic played through the speakers.

'Shall we kick on?' Will asked, voice slurring slightly.

Nate shook his head. 'Nah. I should be getting home. Ang might need a break.'

'Yeah. True. I'd better get my arse home before Kit throws me out,' Will said, with a half-laugh. He didn't miss the look that passed between Nate and Dave.

Dave wrapped an arm around Will's shoulder. 'Come on, mate. I'll drive you home.'

'Nah, it's alright. I haven't had that much.'

'Give us your keys. Mates don't let mates drink and drive,' Dave said. Will could tell he wouldn't win this argument, especially against an ambo who'd probably attended more than his fair share of car accidents in his time.

The lights were out in the cottage as they slowly drove past. Good. He didn't need Tom and Cynthia to know everything he did. The living room light was still on when they reached the homestead. Will thanked Dave, then headed inside. If he woke Kit up, she'd be pissed off, so he lay down on the lounge. Judging by the buzz in his head and the ringing in his ears, he was probably going to feel it in the morning, but it had been a ripper of a night.

✪

Always a light sleeper, Cynthia got to the phone before Tom. She checked the time. 5 am. That and the fear in Kit's voice made her stomach churn. She rustled Tom awake as Kit recounted her eventful night. Her voice cracked, and she sounded as if she were on the verge of a breakdown.

'It's alright. We'll be there in a minute,' she said, looking at Tom, eyes wide.

'What is it? What's wrong?' Tom asked, sitting up.

'Elijah's been crying all night. Kit's in a right state. And Will's out cold on the lounge. She can't wake him.' Tom's expression darkened, then he threw the blankets back and hurried to get dressed, muttering under his breath. Cynthia threw on some clothes, but she couldn't shake the dread in her gut. Tom was usually a placid man, but not when it came to Kit. He'd do anything for his daughter. Will would have some answering to do later, and if it had anything to do with what Cynthia suspected, then they were all in for a bumpy ride.

They walked into the homestead without knocking. Kit was in the kitchen, jiggling Elijah up and down on her shoulder in an attempt to stop his incessant crying. Dressed in her pyjamas, her eyes were bloodshot and surrounded by dark circles. Her hair was a tangled mess, a bird's nest on her head. Cynthia stood in Kit's line of vision and ran her hands up and down her arms.

'It's alright, love,' she said, taking Elijah out of her arms. The volume of his cry increased, but she called over it, 'Grab his bag and get yourself ready. We'll head to the hospital.' Kit stared at her blankly for a moment. 'Go on, love. I've got him.'

With Kit getting organised and Tom nowhere to be seen, Cynthia was determined to give Will a piece of her mind. He lay on the lounge with his legs spread and his head back, mouth agape; the smell of stale beer seeped out of his pores. Cynthia nudged him hard with her knee. How he could sleep through Elijah's cries was anyone's guess.

'Will. Wake up.' His eyelids didn't even flutter. She reached down and pushed his chest. 'Will.' His chest rose and fell in perfect rhythm. Cynthia harrumphed as Kit returned.

'It's no use. He had way too much to drink. Head wetting. What a bloody joke,' Kit scowled. 'It's just an excuse for a boozy night.'

'Never mind that now. Let's go,' Cynthia said. 'Where's your father?' Kit shrugged. Cynthia walked from room to room with Kit trailing behind her and Elijah still crying over her shoulder. She found Tom sitting in the office, shuffling papers. She swallowed the lump in her throat, then turned back to Kit and handed Elijah over. 'Can you go and hop in the car? We'll be out in a sec.' Kit's brow furrowed for a moment before she pivoted. Cynthia turned back to face Tom. He looked up at her, a silent shake of his head conveying his disapproval.

'Someone's moved all of my papers. I can't find anything in here,' he said, pushing the papers around on the desk, making a mess. Cynthia's chest tightened. This was the worst time for Tom to have one of his spells. If Kit saw him, no amount of talking was going to convince her that there was nothing wrong with her dad.

'Alright, hun. We'll sort that out later. We need to go now. Ok?' She eased towards him and placed a hand on his shoulder, hoping that he'd snap out of it before Kit came back. 'Come on. Elijah needs help.' She moved toward the doorway, and he followed. Ignoring Kit's look of confusion, Cynthia sat in the driver's seat while Tom took a spot in the back. Kit sat in the passenger seat and turned around to face Tom.

'What were you doing, Dad?' Kit asked. Cynthia checked his expression in the rearview mirror as she buckled her seat belt. He was staring intently at his phone, clearly ignoring her.

'He was just looking for something. Don't worry about it. We need to get Elijah seen to.'

'You're right. Let's go,' Kit said. Cynthia let out a sigh as she started the car, the engine rumbling to life. If Tom weren't so stubborn about keeping his diagnosis a secret, she wouldn't have to lie to Kit.

The waiting room was empty. They sat on hard plastic chairs and watched the nurses bustling in and out of the rooms. Kit sat, then stood and paced, then sat again, jiggling Elijah the entire time. His cries, though still audible, were growing weaker. Cynthia hoped it was because he'd tired himself out and nothing more serious. Kit's phone rang just as Samantha waved her over. She looked at the screen, then handed it to Cynthia and walked away.

'Kit? Kit? Where are you?' Will's voice called out.

'Nice of you to join the land of the living. We're at the hospital,' Cynthia said. She couldn't hide her feelings. What she could hide was the fact that she'd found a bottle of pills next to her son-in-law. At least for now. There were more important things at stake.

'Why? What's happened? Is Eli alright?'

'Elijah's been crying all night. Kit's very worried about him. She's also not too pleased with you.'

'I'll come into town. Oh, crap! I can't. Dave gave me a lift home.'

'We'll bring your ute back when we come home. I'm sure Elijah will be fine. Kit's in with Samantha now. We'll let you know how it goes. It's probably in your best interest to freshen yourself up before we get home, though, and clean up the floor near the lounge.' She heard movement and then an almost inaudible groan. He knew she knew.

Half an hour later, Kit emerged looking tired but relieved.

'Morning, Mr Brody. Cynthia. I know you've all had a long night, so I just wanted to let you know what the doctor has diagnosed. Baby Elijah has colic. I've explained to Kit that it's unknown what causes it, but the excessive, prolonged crying is a symptom. It might be ongoing for the next few weeks or even months. It's a stressful time for all involved, and Kit will need your support.'

'What can we do?' Cynthia asked.

'There are a few things. Rocking, walking, using white noise, laying him on his belly and rubbing his back, or even a calming bath might work.' Cynthia felt a flood of relief run through her. She'd had a million scenarios running through her head. This was the best outcome.

'Thanks, Sam,' Kit said, then turned back as Sam made her way through the double doors into the corridor beyond the waiting room.

'That's a relief,' Cynthia said. 'It certainly could have been worse.' She handed the phone back to Kit. 'Will wants to speak to you.' Kit scowled and grabbed the phone, then shoved it into her handbag.

Doctor Sunareen came around the corner, nodded at them, then rushed past. Cynthia noticed Tom's muscles loosen for a moment, and then she watched as he steeled himself, jaw tightening.

'Kit, let's grab a coffee,' he said. Kit tilted her head, but agreed. They walked back towards the small cafeteria.

Cynthia knew from Tom's expression what he'd decided to do. She took a seat next to Kit while Elijah slept in the pram next to her. Tom came back from the counter with three coffees. Kit and Tom wrapped their hands around their cups, mirroring each other. Tom cleared his throat and swallowed. Cynthia put her hand on his thigh. He had to do this, but it would not be easy for him. The only thing she could do was show her support.

'I've got some news,' Tom said.

Kit bit her bottom lip. 'You've been different lately, and I couldn't put my finger on it. But I think I've figured it out,' she said. She looked from Tom to Cynthia and back. 'The tool bag, the faraway look, and whatever you were doing in the office last night. I know you've both been trying to hide it. It's dementia, isn't it? Like Grandad had?' Tom and Cynthia nodded in unison. Kit's mouth fell open for a second. Then she got up, unlocked the pram and walked to the car park without another word. Like father, like daughter, Cynthia thought as she and Tom followed Kit outside. At least now they wouldn't have to keep secrets anymore.

'Why did you tell her now, hun?' Cynthia asked Tom before they walked out of the hospital.

He shrugged. 'I don't know. It was like something snapped, and I just thought she had to know. Clearly, she was onto us already anyway.'

'Well, I'm glad you told her, but I probably would have chosen a different time. She's had a rough night.' They stood for a moment in each other's arms. It was done now. There was no turning back.

Kit stood near the car and watched as Tom and Cynthia came through the hospital doors and into the sunlight. Tom held Cynthia's hand and put the other to his eyes to block out the blinding light. He looked the same as he always had. He didn't look like he had dementia. She couldn't just get in the car and drive home with them as if nothing had happened. They'd kept his diagnosis a secret for goodness knows how long. Kit shivered as a surge of frustration ran through her. She turned and walked along the footpath towards Beth's. She spotted Will's car parked outside the pub and let out a snort. He was another problem. He'd been so drunk that he'd passed out. If she couldn't rely on him to be there when she needed him, then what was the point? What was the point of anything?

Beth's bright smile greeted her as Kit opened the door to the café. Beth rounded the counter in record time as soon as she saw the pram.

'Oh my goodness. Is this the little man? What a cutie!' Beth cooed, holding her finger out for Elijah to grab hold of. Beth looked up at Kit, and her smile faded. 'What's wrong, honey?' Kit's lip trembled. Beth led her to a booth. 'You sit right here, and I'll get you something to cheer you up.'

Kit glanced up at a commotion near the door. Jamie, her high school nemesis, waddled inside, heavily pregnant and calling her partner out for not opening the door for her. She was the last person Kit wanted to see after the night she'd had. Kit bent her head and checked her phone. Five messages from Will. Each more urgent than the last. She didn't want to message him back. She wanted him to worry, to hurt as much as he'd hurt her. But no, that wasn't right.

Eli's alright. It was just colic. There. She'd told him their son was alright. That's all he needed to know. He rang, but she declined the call just as Beth returned with two chocolate éclairs. She sat across from Kit and tucked into an éclair.

'Do you want to talk about it?' she asked, wiping her mouth on a serviette. Kit sighed, then shook her head.

'Actually, I'd love a distraction,' she said.

'Say no more. Have I got a story for you,' Beth said with a sly grin. Kit listened as Beth told her about the new man who'd just moved in next door. It sounded as though things were moving quickly. Beth had been single since she'd moved to Sanderson Ridge. She was a lovely lady, and she deserved to be happy. And if this newcomer did that, then Kit was all for it. They finished, and Kit stood up to leave. She leaned over and hugged Beth.

'Thanks. I needed that,' she said.

'Anytime,' Beth said.

As much as she wanted to avoid the confrontation she knew was coming. It was time to head home and face Will. She had a short drive to make a big decision—stand by Will or start again on her own. Was it even as easy as that? What would a divorce be like? Could she raise Elijah on her own? Why was she even thinking like that? She felt completely defeated. She was tired—no, she was exhausted. Her body hadn't felt like her own since she'd become pregnant. Her mind was a jumble, and she couldn't even get the words from her head to her mouth properly. If she wasn't herself. Who was she supposed to be?

Will was sitting on the back verandah. He rose to his feet as she approached him. They stared at each other for a moment before Kit remembered the baby in the pram. She went into the nursery to place him in his cot. She turned to the doorway and stopped. Will was leaning against it, shoulders slumped, mouth turned down, eyes glassy.

'Can we talk?' he whispered. Kit hesitated, torn between her head and her heart. 'Please?' Will held out his hand. She took it and followed him out onto the verandah. She hadn't noticed the flowers on the table before. She sat opposite him and folded her arms. Will sat forward with one hand resting on the table. They locked eyes and held each other's gaze.

'Kit—'

'Will—' They both spoke at the same time. A small laugh eased some of the tension in the air.

'I'm sorry about last night. I didn't know Eli was going to get sick. I just needed to let off some steam.' Will swallowed. His brow knitted together, and he opened and closed his mouth several times. Kit braced herself for the words he might say next. 'I have to tell you something.' Kit's stomach clenched. This was it. Will had decided for her. He looked down at the table, unable to meet her gaze.

'I think I'm addicted to the painkillers I was given when I had the accident.' Kit's jaw dropped. How could she not have noticed? She thought back over the last few months—Will passing out on the couch, his dazed and confused behaviour, the pill bottle always within reach. How could he have been so selfish? How could he have chosen to dull his mind and body right when he was about to become a father? Will looked up, and their eyes met. One glance at his eyes revealed the pain and shame he was enduring. But behind that was the man she'd met in the pub, the man who'd made a fool of himself in front of the whole town trying to ask her to marry him, the man she'd wed, the father of her child, the man she was supposed to spend the rest of her life with.

She got up and went to stand in front of him. 'I'm not going to pretend that I'm not hurt and disappointed because I most definitely am. But you, me, and Elijah are a family now. And we're going to get through this together,' she said. Will stood. He still looked worn out, but he also looked unburdened somehow. Kit let him draw her into his arms. It felt like home.

Chapter 8

Dry Season

Finding the phone number was a breeze, but the decision to click it was harder to make. Will desperately wanted to take some painkillers to get through. It would be so easy to do. The bottle was still sitting on the bench where he usually left it. Then his thoughts turned to what had happened with Elijah the night he'd gotten wasted. He hadn't been there for him or for Kit. With luck, it hadn't been a major issue, but what if it had? He needed to kick the painkiller habit for good. At least if he went about getting clean this way, he could keep the town gossips from knowing. Doctor Sunareen was a fantastic doctor, but Sanderson Ridge was still a small town, and everybody always seemed to find out what was happening in everyone else's lives. People like Mrs Higgins seemed to thrive on bad news. His accident had been on the front page of the local newspaper, and his recovery had appeared on the pages in the following weeks. If Mrs Higgins caught wind of this, it'd be all over town within a few hours. He pressed call, and the phone rang a few times before a man answered.

'Hello. Alcohol and Drug Support Line, how can I help you?' the voice said. Will's throat constricted, and butterflies circled in his stomach. He couldn't do this. 'Is someone there? I'm here to help. What's your name?'

'Will.'

'Hi Will. I'm Paul. How's your day treating you?'

'Could be better,' Will replied.

'I hear you. My six-month-old was up four times last night. I feel like a zombie. Have you got kids?' Paul asked.

'Yeah. A son, Elijah.' Will relaxed onto the kitchen stool as their conversation continued. By the time he disconnected, Paul had managed to calm him enough to get the truth out of him. Paul had filled Will in on what might happen while he was coming off the drugs—mood swings, physical pain, nausea. It sounded much worse than what he'd been enduring since the accident. If he'd known that information before, perhaps he wouldn't have started down this path. Then again, it wasn't like he'd meant to become addicted. It had happened gradually. But now it was time to turn things around.

Will threw the medicine bottle into the bin, then he fished it back out again. He went into the bathroom and emptied the contents into the toilet bowl, flushing the pills away. Immediately, his skin crawled. He couldn't get them back, and he'd already ripped up his last prescription. He had to go cold turkey. Kit's voice drifted down the hallway as she sang lullabies to Elijah. It occurred to Will that it had been a long time since he'd heard her sing. He went into the living room and put his arm around her waist, bending to kiss her neck. She giggled and stepped out of his reach.

'Enough of that,' she said.

'Are you sure? I don't have to work today.' At the mention of work, her face fell. Will tilted his head slightly. 'What is it?'

'I haven't told you what happened at the hospital.' She sat on the lounge and patted the spot next to her. Whatever she was about to tell him wasn't good news. Will braced himself, his heart pounding in his chest. 'Dad told me he has dementia. Well, I kind of figured it out, but he and Cynthia confirmed it.'

'Far out. How long have they known?'

Kit shrugged. 'I haven't really spoken to them about it. I was too peeved that I'd been lied to on top of everything else that happened last night.' Will felt his face grow hot with shame. While Kit had been dealing with their sick child, she'd also found out about her dad having an incurable disease. And all the while, he'd been passed out on drugs and alcohol. His mind jolted back to that day with the tool bag and the dazed look that sometimes came over Tom while they were working.

'I think it's been coming on for a while. Your dad's been forgetting things a bit. He's been repeating stuff that he's already told me too.'

Kit chewed her lower lip. 'Last night he went into the office. Cynthia sent me out to the car, but I thought there was something fishy going on. What if he goes downhill really fast? He might not be here to see Eli grow up or any other grandchildren. I've already lost my mum, and now I'm going to lose my dad.'

Kit's breath came in gasps, and her shoulders trembled as her eyes filled with tears. Will's heart hurt to see her like that and know he couldn't do anything to ease her pain. This time, he wasn't the cause. He moved closer, and she put her arms around his neck and her face to his chest, soaking his shirt in tears. They stayed like that for a while. He listened as she voiced her concerns, though they seemed to circle in an endless loop. He had concerns, too, but now wasn't the time to raise them. Now was the time to support his wife.

'You told me we'd get through my addiction together. This is another thing that we'll get through. I love you, Kit.'

'I love you too,' she said. Will closed his eyes and lifted a hand to rest it on the back of her head. They hadn't said those words in such a long time. The balance of their relationship was shifting.

✪

The smell of roast meat and vegetables wafted from the kitchen out to the back verandah. Tom sniffed the air, then licked his lips and rubbed his stomach. Cynthia giggled and nudged him. Will was sitting on the outdoor lounge with Elijah lying in a rocker on the ground in front of him. They could hear Kit belting out a tune louder than the music streaming from the living room. Will looked up as they approached.

'Look, Eli, Grandad and Grandma are here,' he said with a grin. Tom beamed, making his way over and picking the baby up. It was lovely to see him with his grandchild.

Cynthia snapped a candid photo and sent it to Kit, then held out her hands.

'My turn for a cuddle,' she said. Tom handed Elijah over, and Cynthia went into the kitchen. 'That smells delicious.'

'Thanks. I hope the crackling works out,' Kit said, bending down to look in the oven. She stood up and faced Cynthia. They hadn't seen each other since they had all been standing outside the hospital a few days prior. Tom had wanted to see Kit and explain things, but Cynthia had told him to give her some space. They were both stubborn, and both needed to come to terms with things in their own way. When the dinner invitation had come through, Cynthia had held her phone up with a smug look on her face.

'Dinner will be about twenty minutes. I'll get us a drink, and we can all have a chat,' Kit said, holding up two glasses. Cynthia glanced outside to see Tom and Will already cracking open beers. They sat around the table enjoying the ambience. The sun was still high, the wind was sweeping gently through the gum trees, and the cockatoos were chatting with each other. Elijah gurgled as Will made faces in front of him. Cynthia glanced at Tom, willing him to start the conversation. He got the hint.

'Look, I'm sorry for how you found out about the dementia. I asked Cynthia to keep it quiet, so don't be upset with her. I just needed to get my head around it. Pardon the pun.'

'I just wish you had told me sooner,' Kit said.

'I thought we should tell you, but also, in a way, I agreed with your father. You were dealing with enough with your pregnancy and Will's accident, and his recovery,' Cynthia said. Will looked at the table. Cynthia's eyes darted to Kit. Despite the topic of conversation, she seemed at ease.

'I get that. How long...' Kit paused.

'We've been to see the doc, and we've got a plan. But we'll just take each day as it comes,' Tom said. Kit swallowed and coughed. Cynthia could feel Tom bristle beside her, and she put her hand on his leg under the table. He gave her a weak smile, then looked back at Kit. 'Let's not dwell on the bad when we've got such good things to focus on.' He reached across the table and let Elijah grab hold of his finger. Will sat up straighter.

'Speaking of good things, I wanted to let you both know that I'm off the meds and I don't plan on having any big nights on the grog for a very long time.'

'Good to hear,' Cynthia said, locking eyes with Will and then Kit. Tom, bless his soul, had no idea about Will's overuse of pain medication.

'Excellent, because we've got a busy few weeks ahead, and I'm going to need you to step up when I can't,' Tom said before heading inside. Cynthia sat forward.

'How is it going? I'm guessing you decided to go cold turkey.' Will looked at the door, checking if Tom was within earshot before he answered.

'I did. The first few days were bloody hard. I was sweating like the proverbial, and my mood swings...worse than Kit's when she was pregnant,' he said, trying to lighten the mood. Kit gently punched him in the arm, and he laughed. 'To be honest, I still get an urge. It's like an intense craving or an itch that needs to be scratched. But I've been using a helpline, and Kit's been really supportive. It's early days, but so far, so good.' His eyes darted to the door as Tom came through.

'The CRC's going well. We've got a lot lined up over the next few weeks, so we'll all be busy,' Cynthia said as Tom took his seat. She knew she was keeping something from him, but it wasn't her story to tell.

Daisy, Des, and the other business studies students were waiting outside the CRC when Cynthia pulled up the following Monday. Des helped Cynthia carry in the box of office supplies that she'd picked up from the general store. She apologised for her tardiness, but they brushed it off. While they went into the newly refurbished training room and fired up the computers, Cynthia dumped her handbag on the desk in her office. The headline on the latest issue of the local newspaper caught her eye.

"Local Family Struggles with Illness and Addiction."

She sucked in her breath and read the article. Rose Higgins's unnamed source claimed that Will Stone was so "out of it" at the pub that he could barely stand. Cynthia clenched her fists. Whoever this source was, they'd also felt it was their right to comment on Tom's recent forgetfulness, claiming that he's "suffering just like his father" and that Kit was barely coping with all the stress. It had to be someone of a certain age to remember Tom's father's battle with dementia. The informant also had to have been at the pub the night of the head wetting. Bile rose in Cynthia's throat. She felt woozy and sat down in her chair, her head in her hands. Her shoulders slumped as exhaustion overcame her. She'd tried so hard to hold it together. She'd kept Tom's illness to herself until he was ready to tell Kit. And she'd never mentioned what she knew of Will's painkiller addiction to a single soul. Why had someone hurt her family like this? To make their struggles fodder for the town gossips.

'Hey, the computer's glitching,' Daisy said, walking into the office. Cynthia sat up and sucked in her breath. 'Are you alright?'

Cynthia nodded. 'Certainly,' she said, coming around the side of her desk and ushering Daisy back to the training room. She moved the mouse, turned the computer off and on again, but nothing worked. She was getting more and more annoyed. These machines were new. They shouldn't be having problems. Eventually, she hit the side of the tower, and the computer jolted to life. The students cheered.

'Taking your frustration out on it works a treat, hey?' Desmond said. Cynthia felt her cheeks redden.

'My apologies. I'm a little frazzled at the moment,' she said.

'All good. It can't be easy for you at the moment. You're in the middle of it all,' Daisy said. Cynthia stared at her. Daisy was right. She was caught in the middle of everything that her new family was going through. And now, to top it all off, someone had made their issues front-page news.

When she arrived home, she saw Tom, Will, and Kit standing near the front gate, talking to Rose Higgins. That woman has a nerve showing up here, she thought. Tom greeted her with a kiss.

'Rose wants to hear our side of the story,' he said.

Kit huffed, arms folded. 'She should have done that before putting anything in that rag,' she spat. Tom gave her a stern look. She might be an adult, but he would always be her father. Cynthia didn't blame Kit for her outburst, and she also wouldn't give Rose the satisfaction of a reaction.

'I reported it as it was told to me. There were several witnesses to Will's behaviour,' Rose said. 'If you'd like to make a statement of your own. You know where to find me.' She hopped back into her old Volvo and drove off, leaving them all angry and frustrated.

'Look, it's all out in the open now, and there's nothing we can do about it. So, let's just move on,' Tom said. 'What do you reckon, mate?'

'You're right. Let them think whatever they like. Our mates will still support us,' Will said.

'I understand, but I'm still annoyed that this will be the talk of the town,' Cynthia said, looking at Tom. 'It's been hard enough supporting you through your diagnosis, and trying to help Kit with Elijah, and running the CRC. It's just...' A sob escaped her lips. Tom wrapped his arms around her shoulders and held her head to his chest.

'I'm sorry, sweetheart. You've been there for all of us. I can only imagine how stressed you've been,' he said.

'I'm sorry, too. I'll be more mindful of asking you for things from now on,' Kit said.

'I didn't mean it like that,' Cynthia sighed heavily. 'I've just had a rough day, that's all. Just forget I said anything.' She felt terrible about her outburst. Perhaps the stress of trying to be in control was finally starting to take its toll.

✪

Will was still dressed in his work clothes when he filled the laundry trough with warm water and dropped the small yellow rubber duck in. He had taken more of a hands-on approach with Elijah. After a day that felt like an endless cycle of housework, and feeding and changing Elijah, Kit appreciated the help. She laid the baby on the bench and undressed him as he scrunched his fists and kicked his legs. The sound of his cries reverberated throughout the confines of the small laundry.

'Hey mate. Come on. It's bath time.' Will tried to soothe him, but Elijah wasn't playing his part. The nurses had told Kit that a warm bath would help calm him down. This better work, Kit thought as tension rose in her body. She'd suppressed her frustration all day, but her willpower was reaching its end. She grabbed Will's hand and put it on Elijah's stomach, then walked out of the room. Standing in the hallway with her back against the wall and her eyes closed, she tried the box-breathing exercise she'd read about. In for four counts, hold for four, then out for four. It seemed to work. She waited until the frantic pounding in her chest had

152

subsided before going back into the laundry. Elijah was kicking his legs happily and splashing water over Will.

'You're getting better at this,' she said.

'Practice makes perfect. When he was first born, he was so small. I was worried I'd drop him. Now that he's bulked up a bit, there's more to hold on to.'

'You've bulked up a bit too,' she said with a wink. She took over bathing duties, running warm water over Elijah's belly. Will stared at her and tilted his head to the side.

'Are you alright? Still worried about that article?' he asked. It had been almost a week since the newspaper had come out. They'd had to deal with well-wishers and nosy neighbours wanting to see what was happening for themselves. Kit kept her eyes on Elijah and considered her options. She could tell Will the truth or use the script she'd been telling everyone else.

'I'm fine. Just tired.'

'Okay. Well, don't let it bother you. Your dad and I don't care what some old busybody has to say. Things are far too hectic around here for that. We have to start weaning the calves and moving the cows to the back paddocks.' He let out a weary sigh. 'We need another worker like Vitto. There's too much work for just the two of us at the moment.' Kit wished she could have a hand too. She hadn't realised how all-encompassing being a mother could be. But the worst part was that she had to pretend it wasn't hard at all.

It hadn't even been 24 hours since Elijah's last bout of colic. When he fell silent for a moment, Kit held her breath. Had he finished crying? Was it finally over? Just as her body relaxed, Eli took a deep breath and wailed again, his face turning red with the effort. Kit jiggled him over her shoulder and checked the time. He'd been at it for the last hour, almost non-stop. Anger and frustration formed a knot in her stomach that rose to fill her entire body. She felt hot, wired, and about to explode. She couldn't take it anymore. Marching into Elijah's room, she laid him in his cot, making sure that he was safe. Then she shut the door on her way out. He started crying instantly. Kit felt everything bubble to the surface—frustration, anger, guilt, self-loathing. She ran to her bedroom, threw herself onto the bed, and screamed into her pillow. Curling her body into the foetal position, tears ran down her face; her breath came in short bursts, and her body shook uncontrollably. She knew it wasn't Elijah's fault. He wasn't doing it to upset her. But she wondered how much more she could take.

Kit stretched out on her back, grabbed her phone, and flicked through the photos until she found her favourite. It was a picture of her and her mum, both laughing hysterically at something her dad had done. She couldn't remember what had made them both burst into a fit of giggles, but she vividly remembered how she'd felt—safe, loved, and cared for. If only her mum were still alive, she'd know what to do. She'd probably burst into the room, jump on the bed, smother her in kisses and hugs, and then tell her to suck it up because there was a little boy who needed her.

'Yoohoo,' Cynthia's voice echoed down the hallway. Kit listened as she went into Elijah's room. His crying stopped for a moment, and Kit deduced Cynthia had picked him up. Despite not having children of her own, Cynthia was great with Elijah, and Kit had to admit she turned to her for things, too. Cynthia wasn't her mother, but she was an amazing runner-up. Kit dragged herself up and found Cynthia in the kitchen, humming and jiggling Elijah up and down.

'There you are. I—,' she said, stopping short when she saw Kit's face. She recovered herself and then continued on. 'Was just wondering if you wanted to get out of the house for a bit. I can watch this little man.'

A heavy sigh escaped Kit. 'That would be great. Thank you.' Cynthia waved away her comment and sent Kit out the door.

Kit stood outside with her face turned up to the sun. She could hear Elijah's cries and Cynthia's soothing coos. She opened her eyes and made her way over to the horse stables. Guilt consumed her for a moment when she saw her mare standing under a tree in the paddock next to the stables. Life had been so busy lately that she'd barely had time to look after herself, let alone the animals on the farm. She couldn't see Will and her dad, so she saddled up the horse and rode out to look for them. She ran her hands up and down the horse's neck, feeling its powerful muscles contract as it galloped along the red dirt track. Fresh air filled Kit's lungs, and the sun warmed her back. She felt freer than she had felt in a long time. A broad, satisfied smile spread across her face. When she reached one end of the property, she turned the horse, and together they rode along the far boundary. The farm was large, and it housed a lot of cattle. They hadn't encountered the financial difficulties that had plagued other farmers. There was always a need for beef. But things had changed for them as a family. Tom would not be around as long as any of them hoped, and at some point in the not-too-distant future, he wouldn't have the capacity to help. As much as Will hated it, he was handicapped now. There were so many things that he just couldn't do with one hand. Roustabouts come and go. Local workers tended to move around the different farms, trying to find a better deal. Maybe it was time to make some changes.

Will's ute came into view. Kit slowed the horse to a walk, then stopped and jumped down, patting the horse's shoulder before tying the reins to the fence. Will looked up as she approached.

'What are you doing out here?'

'What? Can't a girl help with farm work?' She said with her hands on her hips. Will raised his hand in surrender.

'I would never say anything like that,' he replied, laughing.

'You look like you mean business, love. What's up?' Tom said. He leaned on the back of the ute and took a swig of water. As if noticing him for the first time, Kit saw the white in his hair, the lines on his face, and the slenderness in his once-muscled arms. She turned and looked back across the paddocks toward the homestead and cottage, which from her vantage point were specks on the horizon.

Will sat on the back of the ute. 'He's right. You've got that look about you.'

Kit pursed her lips. 'You two think you can read me like a book. Well, what am I about to say?' The two men shrugged. 'I want to sell some of the livestock.' Tom's jaw dropped, and Will looked from Kit to her dad.

'Why on earth would we do that?' Tom cried.

'Because, Dad, we have a lot going on. If we reduce the workload, it's going to relieve everyone's stress. I'm sure we can work it out so that we can still keep the farm financially viable but reduce the pressure.'

'I don't know,' Tom said, shaking his head.

'It's just for now. Just until things change.' Like you're not being here, she thought. Kit looked over at Will. He would back her on this. He had to know it was for the best.

'I think I agree with Kit, but I'll go with what you both want to do,' he said diplomatically. He winked at Kit, and they looked at Tom. He gazed out over the paddock and then at the ground. Kit knew what he was thinking. She'd had the same thoughts. But this was the right thing to do.

'If it means that you keep the farm, then let's look into it,' Tom said.

Kit hugged him. 'Thanks, Dad. I knew you'd understand.' Kit could already feel the weight lifting off her shoulders.

Chapter 9

Cynthia had spent a few days pondering how she was going to broach her idea to Tom. He'd either love it or hate it. She decided that Sunday night dinner was the best time. Tom would have a belly full of food and be relaxed after a day off. She placed a bowl of apple pie and vanilla ice cream in front of him and sat down. She waited until he'd taken his first spoonful.

'So, I have an idea,' she said. Tom regarded her as he continued to eat. 'I think we should start a support group for people with dementia and Alzheimer's, and their families. We can hold it at the CRC. It'll just be a casual chat with a cuppa and cake. That sort of thing.' She kept her eyes on him as she ate her own dessert. He was considering it. This was a good sign.

'I don't know about that. I don't really want to share private things.'

'But these people would be going through the same thing as us. They might have ideas on how to handle things as they progress. I would certainly like to chat with other partners.'

'I'll think about it,' he said, then finished the rest of his dessert and turned on the television. The seed was planted. Now Cynthia just had to wait.

She didn't have to wait long. Over breakfast the following day, when Tom had told her to start the group, she'd almost squealed with delight.

Two weeks later, they were both sitting in the front room of the CRC. The wooden floorboards creaked with every step Tom took as he paced back and forth across the room. He sat, then he got up and plucked a biscuit from the table, then he paced again.

'Sit down, hun,' Cynthia said. He stopped and looked at her, worry etched on his features.

'What if no one turns up?' he asked.

'We'll cross that bridge when we come to it,' Cynthia said. Silently, she hoped his fears wouldn't come true. They'd started advertising the Forget Me Not group in the newspaper, right after Rose Higgins' scathing article. They'd also placed flyers at the general store, Beth's, and, of course, in the CRC's front window. She'd had a few inquiries come through, but nothing firm. It had been her idea, and she'd convinced Tom it was going to work. Now he was standing in the front room of the CRC in his best flannel shirt and jeans, stuffing his face with yet another biscuit.

Relief flooded through Cynthia as the doorbell jingled. She went to greet whoever it was, leaving Tom to wipe the crumbs from his shirt.

'This way,' she said, leading the older gentleman and his wife through to the room they'd set up with chairs in a circle.

'This looks like an AA meeting,' the older man said.

Tom let out a nervous laugh. 'That'd probably be easier,' he said.

'Too right. I'm Barry, and this is my wife Mei,' the man said, holding out a hand. Tom made the introductions as a middle-aged woman with blonde hair and a furrowed brow appeared in the doorway. Cynthia waved her in, and they all made cups of tea and coffee before taking their seats. Cynthia sat forward and cleared her throat.

'Thank you all for coming. I trust that you're here for the Forget Me Not group. If not, you might be in the wrong place,' she said before continuing. 'This is just an informal chat. I want everyone to feel comfortable sharing as much or as little as they like about their journey so far.' She sat back, and the room fell silent. She tried to make eye contact with Barry, Mei, and the newcomer, Jane, but they were conveniently looking elsewhere. She turned her attention to Tom.

'Oh, alright.' Tom said begrudgingly. 'I'm Tom. My dad died of dementia, and I've recently been diagnosed with it. I guess I suspected for a while, but I was burying my head in the sand. What we don't know can't hurt us and all that.' Barry nodded in agreement.

'I was the same. Mine's progressing quicker than I hoped, but I'm glad I've got Mei. Good support is invaluable when it comes to this disease,' Barry said. Tom winked at Cynthia. Jane shifted in her seat.

'Jane? Would you like to comment?' Cynthia asked. The fair-haired woman sat with her hands crossed in her lap.

'I don't really have much support,' Jane said, looking at the floor. 'I don't know how I'm going to cope, or how my kids will handle it when things get worse.' Cynthia froze. She couldn't imagine how this woman felt dealing with a diagnosis like this on her own.

'We'll look after you,' Mei said quietly. Jane looked up at Mei and Barry, blinking rapidly.

'Yep. There's not much in the way of services out here. This might be a new group, but I reckon we should stick together,' Barry said. Cynthia felt as if she could burst. This was exactly what she'd pictured when she'd first brought the idea up with Tom. A group of people who could support each other when things were bad and celebrate when things were good. They spent the rest of the meeting discussing medications and coping mechanisms. At the end, after exchanging phone numbers, they all said their goodbyes.

'So much for no one turning up,' she said to Tom when they were sitting in her office.

'Yeah, alright. I'll give you that one,' he said with a wink. Cynthia couldn't wipe the smile off her face, not because she'd won but because they now knew people in their situation. They weren't alone anymore.

★

As Nate scored another goal for the Sanderson Ridge Raiders, Will, Tom, and Desmond cheered from the side of the football oval, their voices hoarse from yelling. Will ached to be on the footy field with his mates rather than relegated to the sidelines with the older men. He knew his first season as a non-player would be hard, but he hadn't realised how much he'd miss the feeling he got when the crowd roared as he took a mark or kicked a goal. He still attempted a friendly kick with the team during training, but it wasn't the same. The Barton Bulldogs midfielder pushed his way through and booted the ball. It sailed towards the goalposts. Will held his breath and then let out a groan as it glided between the poles.

'Bugger,' Desmond muttered, shaking his head.

'How's Fonty Downs treating you?' Will asked Desmond.

'All good. I reckon we'll get a good crop out of this season. Daisy's been doing a course with Cynthia at the CRC so she can do the bookwork.'

'So you reckon you'll be looking for a farm of your own soon?'

'Yeah. I wish I could buy Fonty's,' Desmond said.

'But you work on Fonty's? Didn't you buy it from old Fontlass?' Tom asked, his brow knitted together. Desmond's eyes found Will's, and Will shook his head almost imperceptibly. Desmond drew his eyes to the field.

'Did you see that? What a tackle!' he exclaimed. They all watched on as Nate fought his way out of the scrum and handballed the footy to Dave, who darted between players and kicked it towards their goals just as the siren sounded. It missed, and the crowd groaned collectively. The Bulldogs had won 89-76.

'We'll get them next time,' Tom said, glancing around. 'I'd better go find Cynthia. She's probably had a few champers in the ladies' lounge.'

Will turned to Desmond after confirming Tom was a safe distance away.

'Thanks for that,' he said.

'Daisy read about his dementia in the newspaper. Is he like that all the time now?'

Will shrugged his shoulder. 'It comes and goes. It'll get worse over the next few months and years if he gets that far.'

Desmond shook his head. 'Shame. He's a top bloke. As if that family hadn't been through enough already. You know Daisy and I are just next door if you need anything.' Will thanked him and headed for the clubrooms. The mood would be sombre. The players were grumbling about the umpires' calls and the dirty tactics of the opposition. Will commiserated with them. After seeing Tom make another misstep, he wasn't in the mood to party anyway.

By the time Monday rolled around, Will was determined to lift his game. Running the cattle farm was hard yakka, and Tom needed his help to make it work. He spent the day, the sun warm on his skin, completing his tasks as best he could. He'd become rather inventive. If he couldn't do things the way he used to, he found new ways of doing them. Like using his feet to hold things in place, or teaching the dogs to shut the gates. That one had taken weeks to master, but now he had worthy sidekicks.

The cows shuffled their way through the gate and into the next paddock. Will followed along in his ute. The sun was setting, but this was the last job for the day, and he was determined to get it done. The last cow was taking its time, meandering as if it had all the time in the world. He got out and whistled for the dogs to give him a hand. The cow wandered through the gate, and the dogs nudged it shut. Will still had to latch it. He didn't think they could manage that part. Squinting in the low light, he walked back to the car, tripped on a rock and stumbled, putting his left hand out to catch his fall. His right arm flapped forward but did nothing to support his weight. He fell heavily onto his right side, the rough ground scraping his skin as he cursed loudly. He struggled to his knees and climbed into the driver's seat of the ute. Wincing in pain, he rubbed his aching shoulder. His mood was darker than the sky by the time he made it back to the homestead.

'What's up?' Kit asked as soon as he walked in.

'Nothing. My shoulder's killing me,' he said, pushing past her and going into the bathroom to wash up. He washed his grazed hand and splashed his face. His eyes honed in on the painkillers Kit used when she had cramps. The tablets were nowhere near as strong as the medication he'd been on. The last time he'd spoken with Paul on the support line, he'd explained that taking even one tablet could send Will straight back to where he was, especially since he was newly clean and sober. Surely he could take a couple to ease the pain without relapsing? It was mind over matter, right? A powerful urge swelled inside him. He needed to have them, for better or worse. The compulsion was so strong that it blocked out all other thoughts. The pain was intense, and the fix was in his hand. All he had to do was pop open the packet and swallow a pill or two.

'Hey, babe, dinner's ready,' Kit said from outside the door.

'Coming,' he called over his shoulder. He couldn't draw his eyes away from the packet now in his hands. Would Kit know if any were missing? What if he told her he'd taken them? Then it wouldn't be a secret. They weren't even strong. Kit started singing, and her voice drew him back.

'No. I can't,' Will muttered, his voice a low rasp. The packet crinkled as he returned it to its place. A cold sweat prickled his skin; he would win, not the addiction, not this time. He looked in the mirror. 'You're stronger than this,' he said. As he headed towards the dining room, Elijah's giggle echoed down the hallway. He would do this for himself, but other people needed him too.

✪

Though the morning air was cool, the sun's rays promised sweltering heat before long. The fresh air would do both Kit and Elijah good. She pushed the pram over to the paddock where the horses were kept. She called to her horse, and it came running, its brown mane flowing as it trotted over to the fence. The chestnut horse whinnied and snorted. Elijah let out a loud giggle. Kit felt as if her chest expanded with love. She didn't realise how much love she would or could feel until she'd had Elijah. She knew she loved him, but if she was being honest with herself, she also disliked him. No, not him; his behaviour. The incessant crying, the waking up at all hours. She thought she'd prepared herself for it. Sometimes, she wished she weren't a mother. Then he'd smile up at her with that infectious little giggle, and she'd feel a surge of happiness, quickly followed by a sense of guilt.

'You like that, huh? Are you going to be a cowboy like your daddy when you grow up?' she said, tickling him under his chubby chin.

'I'm not exactly a cowboy,' Will said, coming up behind her. He laid his left hand on the fence, but his eyes were on her. 'You look happy today.'

In the face of the sunny sky and the love she'd felt, something deep within her clicked. She turned to Will, her stern face a mask of determination.

'I have to tell you something.' Will's smile faded. 'You've noticed that I haven't been happy lately. Well, I've been struggling. With the pressure of knowing we have to keep this farm running, with Dad's illness, and finding out about your addiction. But mostly with Eli. Don't get me wrong. I love him so much. But it's been hard.' Her voice trailed off. What else could she say? Will chewed the side of his cheek.

'Do you want a solution, or do you want to vent?' he asked.

'Where did you pick that line up? Oprah?'

He rolled his eyes. 'No. From Paul on the helpline.'

Kit thought for a moment. Why had she finally told him how she'd been feeling? 'I want a solution.'

Will slapped his hand on the fence post. 'Good answer. I think you need to go see Samantha at the hospital. She's probably dealt with this sort of thing before.'

'I don't know if I can talk to someone else about it.'

He raised his eyebrows. 'Talking is what's helping me get through my stuff. It really does help.' She tilted her head. 'Look, I'll admit I've struggled. But talking to Paul has been the best thing to help me deal with it all. As for the farm, we'll work something out. We always do.'

Two hours later, Kit walked out of the hospital doors feeling much lighter than she had when she'd walked in. Will had been right. Samantha had dealt with this before. She'd been so respectful and caring. It was hard to reconcile her with the bully she used to be. Kit grinned as Jamie squeezed out of the back seat of a car carrying her newborn daughter. Why were small towns the gift that kept on giving? Jamie had been the ringleader of the high school clique. She and Angela had reconciled their differences a few years ago, but Kit had yet to put that water under the bridge with her. Now they were both new mums. Perhaps Jamie was feeling the same way she was. She met her at the hospital entrance.

'Hey, Jamie. You got a sec?' Jamie checked her smartwatch and nodded. 'I'm thinking of starting a mother's group. Would you be interested in coming?' Kit asked, glancing down at the bundle swaddled in a pink blanket. Jamie tilted her head slightly and stared at her for a moment.

Was she ready to settle things, or would she continue with the way they'd dealt with each other for years?

'If I can get out of the house, then yeah, sounds good.'

Kit let out a breath and smiled. 'Great. I've got to run it by Cynthia. I'll let you know.' The first step was taken. She already knew Cynthia would be on board. She and her dad had had success with their dementia group recently. As Kit strapped Elijah into his car seat, she snorted and shook her head. In the space of a few hours, she'd gone from not wanting to talk to anyone about how she felt to starting a mother's group. Will and Cynthia's influence was clearly rubbing off on her.

Chapter 10

In the restaurant, connected to the pub, the air buzzed with the lively chatter of patrons and the light sounds of cutlery clinking on plates. Will's nostrils flared as the smell of chicken parmigiana hit him. He pushed the pram closer to the table and took a seat next to Kit. Tom and Cynthia both turned their attention to Elijah, who lapped it up with a big, toothless grin. Kit put a hand on Will's leg and squeezed gently. The physio he'd been seeing online had given him exercises that not only made his working arm stronger but also helped build more muscle over his entire body than he'd ever had before. Kit had been appreciative of his efforts. Helping Elijah was a lot easier now, too. Will winked at Kit and then checked the menu. He always did, even though he knew he'd end up getting the parmy and pint special, only this time he'd give the pint to Tom and have a cola instead.

'It's so good to have a family dinner like this,' Cynthia said, beaming. Tom put his arm around her shoulder and kissed the top of her head. Kit groaned and then grinned.

'Get a room, you two,' she joked, the levity in her voice vanishing as she turned serious. 'We still need to make a plan for the farm.' The jovial mood evaporated, replaced by a palpable tension. Why did she have to bring it up now? They'd deal with it when they needed to. Will shifted in his seat and waved to Nate as he followed Angela, pushing Ethan in the pram, into the restaurant.

'Leave it for now, love,' Tom whispered as they approached the table.

'G'day,' Nate said. 'Mind if we join you?'

Will glanced at the others, who all shook their heads. 'The more the merrier,' he said. Kit, Angela, and Cynthia fussed over the babies. Tom, Nate, and Will turned to discussing how the Sanderson Ridge Raiders had played the day before.

'I can't believe we lost to Merredin. We've got to win the next game, or we won't make the finals,' Nate said.

'Yeah. With Davies and McGregor out, we weren't on our game. We'll stick to the Tigers, don't you worry about that,' Will said.

'Tigers...I thought we were playing Merredin,' Tom said. Will eyed Nate and mouthed the words 'leave it'. They were saved from correcting Tom by the waitress bringing their order. In between dinner and the next round of drinks, Nate caught Will's attention.

'I bought a new toolbox. Do you want to check it out?'

'Boys and their toys,' Kit said, shaking her head. Angela sniggered. Will stuck his tongue out at Kit, then followed Nate out. They stood leaning against the sides of the ute tray, admiring Nate's new toolbox, which sat near the cab and ran the width of the ute tray. Will knew they weren't out there to discuss Nate's new accessory.

'Sorry about what happened in there. We've been told it's better not to correct Tom too much.'

'His memory is fading quickly, isn't it?' Nate asked.

Will took a deep breath. 'Yeah, it is. Kit's keen to sell some stock to ease the load a bit, but even doing that's a lot of work.' Will shrugged. 'That's life, hey. We'll sort it out.'

'Nah. We don't leave our mates hanging when they need a hand. Leave it with me,' Nate said. Will shook his head and told Nate they'd sort it out. He was just venting. He didn't want to spoil the evening. They headed back inside and joined their families for dessert. Kit eyed him, and he winked at her. She grinned and returned his wink.

Back at the homestead, Elijah was sleeping in his own room, and Kit and Will lay on their bed. Kit's leg bent over Will's, and her hand was on his chest.

'So how was Nate's toolbox?' she said teasingly.

'You know I'd rather not be thinking about Nate right now.'

Kit laughed. 'Let me give you something else to think about then.' She ran her hand down his chest, and everything else left his mind.

Two days later, Will was brushing his teeth in the bathroom when a horn beeped. He looked up as Kit appeared in the doorway, eyebrows raised. He shrugged his shoulder, and they walked out the front door and stood on the verandah. Elijah was happily gurgling in the sling wrapped around Kit's midsection. His colic episodes seemed to hit more in the early evening nowadays. Kit referred to it as the witching hour. It had certainly felt like it the night before when Elijah had screamed until his face went red. Kit had been so strong, taking deep breaths and trying to soothe him, but Will had needed to go outside to calm himself down. Now, the baby boy was behaving as if nothing had happened. Will leaned down and planted a kiss on his forehead.

'What's going on?' Kit asked.

'No idea.' Will said as they walked hand in hand over to where Nate, Angela, Kane, Charlotte, Daisy, and Desmond were standing.

'Now that we're all here, let's crack on,' Nate said. He started delegating tasks, and the others murmured in response.

'What's going on, mate?' Will asked him. Nate clapped him on the back with a booming laugh.

'You guys need help. This is what we do around here,' he said. 'Let's start with a cull.' They jumped into the truck and headed for the paddock where the older cattle were kept. Tom pulled up in his ute minutes later, grateful for the assistance and thankfully running on all cylinders. While the trio rounded the cattle up and loaded them into the back of the truck. The others spent the morning branding and tagging cattle and moving some of the herd to paddocks where there was more feed. It would have taken Tom and Will at least a week to do the work that their friends and neighbours had helped them do in the space of a few hours. Now, all they had to do was offload the stock.

✪

Cynthia looked out the kitchen window of the cottage. The sun was high in the sky, and the temperature was a balmy 35 degrees. The help they'd had from Nate, Angela, Kane, Charlotte, Daisy, and Desmond had seemed to spur Tom on. After putting on a BBQ lunch as a thank you, the group headed to their respective farms. Cynthia hadn't seen Tom for a few hours, so she called Kit.

'Dad's gone with Will and Nate to the auction,' Kit said. Cynthia froze. Tom hadn't said goodbye. He always kissed her before he left. Was he having an episode? It was too risky not to check. What if he said the wrong thing or wandered off and got lost? Her mind raced with possibilities as she drove into town.

By the time she reached the cattle yards on the outskirts of town, the auction had already started. She spotted Tom, Will, and Nate standing near the railing. Tom was leaning over with one foot perched on the bottom rail. He looked fine. Perhaps he'd just been in a rush and had forgotten to see her before he'd left. Cynthia moved next to him, and he smiled at her.

'What are you doing here?'

'I was in the area.' She replied as the auctioneer started the bidding on part of their herd. The bids were coming thick and fast, and before anyone knew it, Tom had raised his hand to bid. Will nudged him in the side, and he lowered his hand, a confused look on his face.

'They look alright. Let's bid before someone else gets them,' he whispered urgently.

Will shook his head. 'They're ours. We're not bidding on our own cattle.' Tom's face drained of colour, and he swayed back a step, nearly losing his balance. Cynthia put a hand out to grab his arm.

'It's alright, hun. Let's see what happens,' she whispered, gripping him. They waited as the auctioneer called for final bids. Cynthia breathed a sigh of relief as another farmer raised his hand. She could smooth over this minor mistake if anyone mentioned it. The auctioneer came over to see them and confirm the sale price.

'I nearly sold you your own cattle, Tommy. What the heck were you doing?'

'Just testing you out, Simmo,' a voice behind them said. Cynthia and Tom turned to see Barry from their forget-me-not group standing behind them with his Akubra tipped in their direction. The auctioneer snickered and then turned his attention to the next lot to be auctioned off. Barry steered Tom and Cynthia away from the crowd.

'You right, mate?' he asked Tom.

Tom swallowed hard and nodded. 'It was just a slip-up. Thanks for stepping in.'

'Don't worry about it. We all have them,' Barry said with a wide grin. 'Well, I'd better be getting home before I buy something I don't need and Mei threatens to leave me again.' His laughter shook his enormous belly as he headed towards the car park. Tom's shoulders were slumped, and he kept his eyes on the ground. Cynthia's stomach twisted with a familiar dread. She hated seeing him like this.

'Let's get out of here,' Cynthia suggested, grabbing his hand. They were quiet as they made their way down the main street of Sanderson Ridge. With the auction on, the town was busier than usual. Cars were lined up on both sides of the street. They walked past the pub and the CRC and ended up outside the cemetery gates. Tom led them to the bench, and they faced each other.

'It doesn't seem like that long ago that I brought you here to tell you I loved you,' Tom said.

'Yes, it was such a romantic spot to do that,' Cynthia said, rolling her eyes and smirking.

'Well, I am a romantic guy.' Cynthia burst out laughing, but quietened when she looked at Tom's face. He wasn't in a joking mood anymore. A knot formed in her stomach. Was he going to call things off? Did he not want to be with her anymore? He looked at his feet and shuffled them in the gravel, then he took a deep breath. Cynthia braced herself.

'I know this bloody disease is progressing quicker than we thought it would. I feel like I'm losing my mind. I am, really.' Tom raised his head and looked across the road at the CRC. 'I feel like things are slipping away, and I want to hold on to what I can. Little Elijah is pretty bloody special. And Kit means the world to me. I'm so glad she's found Will. He's not perfect, but none of us are. And then there's you. You've changed my life for the better. I couldn't imagine living whatever time I have left without you. Will you marry me?' he asked. The knot in Cynthia's stomach evaporated, and she stared at him, mouth agape. 'Are you actually speechless for once? I just asked if you'll marry me.'

Cynthia recovered enough to answer him. 'I wasn't expecting it. That's all. I mean, look where we're sitting.'

'Well, I wasn't about to get down on one knee on that gravel. I'd never get back up.'

She playfully slapped his leg, then turned serious. 'Are you sure?' she asked.

He nodded. 'I'm certain. I love you. And if you'll accept what's coming, then I'd be honoured to be your husband. But I need you to think about it. I mean, with the dementia and all.'

'I don't need to think about it. I'm absolutely sure. I've waited a lifetime for this.' She melted into his arms and sealed the moment with a kiss. When they pulled apart, Tom added. 'I haven't organised a ring either. I thought you'd be better at picking out one you liked.'

'You know me well,' she said, leaning in for another kiss.

The sale yards were emptying by the time they got back. Will and Nate stood near the truck. Their conversation stopped when they saw Cynthia and Tom approach. Cynthia felt a pang of worry and hoped that Tom hadn't noticed. By the way, he sidled up to Will with a grin on his face; he hadn't. Cynthia was glad he was a less-than-observant man.

'We've got some news.' Will glanced at her for a moment, and when she grinned, he visibly relaxed. 'It looks like the little woman and I are going to make things official,' Tom announced. Will and Nate, grinning widely, slapped him on the back with a resounding thwack.

'Congrats, mate. You too, Cynthia. I'm glad you're making an honest man out of him,' Will said, leaning in to hug her.

'When's the wedding?' Nate asked.

'Whoa,' Tom said, hands raised. 'We haven't got that far yet.'

They'd only just decided to marry, but at their age, and with Tom's diagnosis, why wait?

'There's no point putting it off, though. Stay tuned for your invitations, boys,' Cynthia said. Tom looked at her wide-eyed, and she shrugged a shoulder. She knew she'd get him on board with the plan. A wedding was the perfect antidote to months of stress the family had endured, something to look forward to that held the promise of happiness.

✪

The babies lay on a blanket together, kicking their little feet in the air and gurgling to each other while their mothers sat at the table nearby. Cynthia had been on board with the idea of a mother's group from the minute Kit mentioned it. She'd put a notice in the newspaper and stuck flyers in the front windows of the local shops. Charlotte had mentioned it to anyone who entered the general store with a young child. Their efforts had paid off. Five mothers were sitting around the table enjoying a cuppa and chat. Kit, next to Angela, lifted the plate of biscuits and passed it around.

'Mrs Higgins mentioned your dad has some medical issues,' Jamie said, taking a biscuit. 'I hope everything's alright.' Kit eyed her for a second. Was she being genuine? It was hard to tell with Jamie. Kit thought everyone in town knew about her dad's illness after the article in the newspaper. Jamie had probably been too focused on her own pregnancy.

'He's got dementia. We're all just taking it day by day,' Kit answered.

Jamie cast her eyes down. 'I'm sorry to hear that,' she said. Her condolences felt honest, but Kit didn't want to discuss her dad today. To her relief, Angela coughed and changed the subject.

'So, is anyone getting any sleep, or am I the only one who feels like the walking dead?' she said. The other women laughed. All the mothers had the same issues—not much sleep, and no idea if they were doing this mothering thing right. Thoughts were bubbling up in Kit. What if the other women felt like they'd lost themselves, too? She straightened in her chair.

'I feel like I'm not the same person anymore, like I've lost who I am.' Kit cringed as the silence stretched on, thick and heavy. Had she said the wrong thing? Was she the only one with these thoughts? Angela leaned closer to the table.

'You're not the same person.' Kit froze, and Angela continued. 'None of us are. We're mums now. And we have to find out who we are in this new phase of our lives.' She lifted her mug. 'To discovering ourselves again.' The other women followed suit. Relief flooded through Kit. Sarah, an older mum and newcomer to town who'd found out about the group through Charlotte, put her cup down and looked directly at Kit.

'You've got to do the things that you love. Even if it's just a few minutes a day. Read a book. Belt out a tune. Dig in the garden. Whatever it is, carve out some time every day just for yourself. It does wonders for your mental health. Our babies pick up on our moods, so being calm and happy means that our babies are calm and happy.' She smiled encouragingly. Kit felt seen, as though every woman in that room understood her hidden emotions. When the others left, Kit hung back to help clean up.

'How did it go?' Cynthia asked, coming into the room to help.

'Really good. I feel so much better than I did a month ago.'

'I'm glad, because there's something I want to ask you.' Kit sighed inwardly. She'd only just got her head in the right space, and now someone wanted something from her. It always happened that way. 'Now, don't look so worried. It's nothing bad. I was just wondering...if you would be my maid of honour.'

Kit rushed forward and put her arms around Cynthia's neck. 'Of course I will.' She couldn't think of anything that would make her happier than to see her dad and Cynthia get married. She'd seen the way Cynthia had made room in her life for Kit, Will, and now Eli. Cynthia had accepted her dad's illness and was helping him tackle it head-on. Kit had a feeling that Cynthia was going to be in her life, even after her dad left it.

Elijah was fast asleep in the sling wrapped around Kit's middle while she carefully dodged the chickens that ran around under her feet, clucking their annoyance at her intrusion into their space. She could see Will standing near the back of his ute, talking on his phone. Her dad and Cynthia were walking towards the homestead hand in hand. She put the eggs into the sling and shut the chook pen door behind her.

'I'll just pop these inside,' she called to Will, and he waved an acknowledgement. When she returned, sans Elijah, who would hopefully sleep for Cynthia for the next few hours, she jumped into the ute next to Will and cranked up the stereo. As they made their way into town, she sang along to the radio at the top of her lungs while Will joined in for the chorus. The music from the pub hit them before they got inside. Kit made a beeline for the DJ booth while Will dodged his way through the crowd to their group of friends standing in the far corner. Angela, Nate, Charlotte, and Kane were watching from their vantage point, ready to show their support.

'I haven't done this in quite a while, so please bear with me,' Kit said, standing in front of the microphone in a red A-line dress, her dark hair pulled up in a high ponytail. The first few bars of The Horses started, and the mood shifted. Darryl Brathwaite's classic always got the crowd pumped up. Kit was back in the swing of things in no time, dancing around, belting out the songs with her powerful voice. She sang three more songs and then told the crowd she'd be taking a break.

'That was brilliant, sweetheart,' Will said, handing her a drink. Kit's body tingled with adrenaline and endorphins, and she swung her arms around Will's neck, nuzzling into him and pulling him onto the dance floor. Will didn't mind the ribbing he got from the other men when they returned to the group after the song ended.

'It's so good to have a night out,' Kit said. Angela raised her glass in agreement. With Elijah and Ethan now sleeping through the night and starting on solid foods, life had become a little bit easier.

'Are things settled on the farm now?' Angela asked her.

'Yeah. Having all of you help out was just what we needed. It's like a weight has been lifted off all our shoulders,' Kit said.

'That's good to hear,' Nate said. 'Swings and roundabouts. I'm sure there'll come a time when you guys can lend a hand to someone else.' That was true. Sanderson Ridge might feel stifling sometimes, but everyone was willing to help when someone needed it. Kit remembered when Angela needed help to build the station stay. Everyone pitched in to get it finished in record time, and now their business was thriving.

The DJ started playing a Pink song, and Kit and Angela smirked at each other before shimmying their way back onto the dance floor.

'Thanks for organising things with Shirley. I think I needed that extra push to get back up there,' Kit said, pointing to the stage. Angela grinned and swung her around. It felt just like old times. After another round of singing, Angela and Nate started yawning. Then everyone else followed suit. Whoever said yawning was contagious was absolutely right. As the group walked back to their cars and said goodnight, Kit felt exhausted, but she also felt more like herself than she had in months.

Chapter 11

The young man standing next to the battered four-wheel-drive was dressed in a clean, checked shirt and jeans, a wide-brimmed hat covering his cropped dark hair. Will had watched him get out of his car with a mixture of trepidation and hope. It had been a week since the night out at the pub, but it had been a success in more ways than one. Not only had Kit got back on stage, but he had spread the word about needing a new farmhand. Will stepped down off the verandah and felt the man's eyes on him. He shifted subtly to compensate for his immobile arm. The man stared at him for a moment before looking towards the paddocks.

'You're Daisy and Des's boy, yeah?' Will asked.

'Maali,' the man answered. 'I heard you had some work going here.'

'We do, if you reckon you're up to it,' Will said.

'I can work harder than most of the whitefellas in town,' Maali said with a straight face before breaking into a grin.

'Alright. Come on then. Let's see what you can do.' The two men jumped into the back of the ute.

'Tom not working today?' Maali asked. Will bit the side of his cheek.

'Nah. It's just the two of us. He's feeling a bit under the weather.'

'Dad told me about his illness.' Will nodded but said nothing more. They reached the gate, and Maali jumped out and opened it, making sure it was closed behind him. It was a good sign. The two men worked hard for a few hours before heading back to the homestead for morning tea.

Tom was sitting on the rocking chair on the back verandah of the homestead, looking out across the paddocks. Will halted for a split second, then recovered and greeted him.

'Looks like we've got ourselves a new employee,' Will said to Tom, then glanced over at Maali. Tom eyed the young man for a moment.

'You look like someone I used to know. His name was Desmond.'

Maalia didn't miss a beat. 'That's my dad. Everyone tells me I'm the spitting image of him.' Tom tilted his head and knitted his eyebrows. Will watched his face transform as recognition dawned.

'You're Maali. I remember when you were this big,' Tom said, holding a hand about a metre from the ground. He shook his head. 'It doesn't seem that long ago.'

'Time flies, Mr Brody,' Maali said.

'Don't Des and Daisy own Fonty's? Why aren't you working for them?' Tom asked.

Maali shook his head. 'They work it, but they don't own it. I can't work for my dad. I just can't.'

Tom let out a laugh. 'I hear you. Working with my old man was bloody frustrating sometimes.'

Kit brought out muffins and coffees and the men worked out the terms of Maali's employment as they ate. Will peered over at Tom. It had been a tough year for him, but the older man was still cracking jokes. How long would he be able to sit and have a conversation with him? How long before Tom forgot who he was? Will shook the thoughts from his head. If moments like this were dwindling, then he wanted to be present for what was left of them. He twisted in his seat to grab his drink and felt a sharp stab of pain in his shoulder. His immediate thoughts went to painkillers. He took a measured breath and swallowed. No, this sort of thing was going to happen. Paul and the other counsellors on the helpline had warned him this would happen. It was mind over matter. As he reached for his drink a second time, he ignored the niggling pain. He was in control, and he planned to stay that way for the rest of his life.

★

The back verandah of the CRC was lined with rows of chairs, and a lectern made by the local men's shed stood at the front. Cynthia went back and forth, placing a program on each chair. She'd just finished the last row when the first guests arrived.

'Welcome. Take a seat wherever you like,' she called out as she went back inside to grab the certificates from her office. She looked up at the knock on her door. Daisy Jurrah stood in the doorway wearing a bright green and white polka dot dress and a broad grin.

'Daisy, you look lovely.' Cynthia came around the desk. 'Are you all set?'

'Yep. My mob is ready and waiting.' The two women walked back out onto the verandah. The seats were filling up fast, and Cynthia worried she hadn't set out enough. She turned to Daisy and instructed her to gather the other students and sit together in the front row. Her head was running a mile a minute, but Cynthia felt a rush of excitement. A flash popped in her eyes, and she looked up to find Angela pointing a camera in her direction. She stood taller and struck a pose.

'Thank you for agreeing to take the photos,' Cynthia said.

'Anytime. I think it's fantastic that you've set this up. It's just what we needed. With any luck, it'll help the Ridge grow bigger and better,' Angela said. Cynthia thanked her and then took her spot at the lectern. The seats were filled, and people were standing at the back. She cleared her throat and began the ceremony.

She'd made sure Daisy's certificate was the last in the pile. When she called out her name, a large part of the crowd let out a cheer. As Daisy made her way to the stage, Cynthia continued.

'Daisy Jurrah was the first student to enrol here. I want to congratulate her not only for finishing her course but for having the courage to sign up in the first place. Higher education can be a challenge for anyone, but Daisy took that challenge on with gusto. I want to say a special thank you to her for trusting me.' Cynthia's voice broke, and Daisy whispered 'you've got this' as encouragement. Cynthia smiled up at her, then passed her the certificate and shook her hand. 'Congratulations, Daisy!' Everyone clapped, cheered, and whooped. Daisy held up her certificate, and Angela snapped more photos. Cynthia had pictured this moment when the opportunity to take on tertiary learning presented itself, and now it had come to fruition. As she watched her first group of graduates stand together and take a bow, she wiped a tear from her eyes.

Tom pulled her aside with a grin on his face.

'Guess what?' he said. Cynthia looked at him with her eyebrows raised, waiting. 'After the wedding, we're honeymooning in Europe. Kit helped me book the flights and organise everything.' Cynthia let out a squeal. The wedding was only weeks away, and now they'd get to see the world together. Everything was finally falling into place.

✪

Kit pushed Elijah in the pram with Will at her side. Tom and Cynthia were walking hand in hand a few strides in front. They entered the beer garden at the back of the pub and found a table under a gazebo. It was a warm day, and Kit lifted her head to catch the spray from the mister lining the roof of the gazebo.

'You look like you need a drink,' Shirley said as she approached the table.

'Definitely. I love not breastfeeding,' Kit said with a chuckle.

'I've been meaning to catch up with you. How do you feel about doing some sundowners out here? Nothing fancy. Just your amazing voice and some music in the background.'

Kit glanced at Will. 'It's your call, babe. Eli and I will be your groupies,' he said. Kit took a second to consider her options. She loved singing. If there was one thing that made her feel like herself, it was singing. Elijah's colic seemed to have passed, and he was growing at a rapid pace. Now that Maali was on the farm, Will was almost back to his old self. Maybe now was the right time.

'I'm in,' she said, nodding.

'Excellent. When can you start?' Shirley asked.

'Whenever you're ready.'

'How about now?'

It only took a split second for Kit to consider it before she was heading inside to grab the audio equipment.

The beer garden was at half capacity, but that didn't stop Kit from giving it her all. She sang a few numbers, then told the crowd she needed five. She came back with a guitar in her hand. Sitting on the bar stool, back straight, fingers ready to pluck and strum, Kit looked over at Will. He gave her a thumbs-up as he pointed his phone at her to video her performance. Kit closed her eyes and lost herself to the music as she sang an original song. She'd written it when she was a teenager. Writing songs was her way of dealing with the pain of losing her mum. But she'd never performed them until now.

'That was incredible. I've never heard it before,' Will said as Kit took her seat next to him.

'It's mine,' she said, fixing her gaze on Elijah so that she didn't see Will's reaction. She couldn't bear it if he said it was good but actually thought it was crap.

'No kidding,' he said. He fiddled with his phone, then laid it in his lap. 'Done,' he said.

'Done what?' Kit asked him, head tilted. He gave her a sly grin, and she narrowed her eyes at him.

'Done as in done posting it on YouTube.'

Kit's jaw dropped. 'Are you serious? I can't...It's not ready—' Will put a finger to her lips.

'Let's let the public decide.'

'Will Stone, you cheeky bugger. If that tanks, I'm blaming you,' Kit said. Will pulled her close and planted a kiss on her lips.

'It won't tank. Trust me,' he said, then kissed her again.

'Alright. Alright. Enough of that, you two,' Tom said with a laugh. While they finished their drinks, Kit's mind was on the possibilities. People were so cruel in the comments section on social media. She might put on a brave face, but she didn't have thick skin. If anything, she hoped nobody saw the video. Then she would have nothing to worry about.

Epilogue

One month later

The flower-adorned arbour had been set up under the tree; the chairs, filled with their family and friends, were laid out in neat rows, and the priest stood at the end of the aisle flicking through his bible. Tom wrung his hands, then wiped them on his black suit pants, then ran them through his hair. Cynthia felt the same nervous tension running through her body as she followed Kit behind the last row of chairs and into the middle of the aisle. They'd spent the morning getting their hair and makeup done in the homestead, while Will and Tom had taken over the cottage. Her dress, which had been ordered from Perth, only arrived the day before, but thankfully, it fit her perfectly. Kit looked gorgeous with her hair flowing down her back in soft curls. Cynthia could only describe the feeling she felt when looking at Kit as pride. It was the same feeling she had when she took Elijah with her to the CRC and showed him off to everyone who came in.

Soft instrumental music streamed from a speaker, and Tom turned to look in her direction. A look of pure joy bloomed on his face. She felt it too as she stood in front of him and looked into his dark brown eyes. Her voice faltered as she recited her vows, and a tear flowed down Tom's cheek as he said his. Before she had time to process it, the ceremony was over, and they were signing the official papers. Everyone cheered as they walked down the aisle for the first time as husband and wife. It had been years in the making, but it was more special now than it would have been if they had wed when they were teenagers.

'You look stunning,' Tom said as they paced around the floor of the marquee.

'You scrub up alright yourself,' Cynthia said with a wink. 'Can we do this when we're in London or Paris?'

'Absolutely,' Tom said. Cynthia laid her head on his chest and closed her eyes, fully present in the most perfect moment of her life.

✪

The air was warm, and the sun was about to hit the tip of the ridge off in the distance. Tom and Cynthia had been gone for a week. They video-called from whichever little English village they happened to be in at the time and told them they planned to visit Paris in a few days. With Maali's help, Kit and Will had finished work early and were enjoying some family time on the back verandah. Elijah kicked his legs, and his bouncer jostled up and down at their feet. Kit reached over and tickled his tummy, eliciting a giggle that made his parents grin. Will handed her a glass, then took a seat and let out a long, slow breath.

'This has been a hell of a year, and I wouldn't wish some of the stuff we went through on my worst enemy, but we got through it. Thanks for putting up with me. It can't have been easy,' Will said.

'The year certainly didn't go as planned. That's for sure. It was bloody hard at times and, if I'm honest, there were times when I wasn't sure we'd make it through together. And I'll be the first to admit that I struggled with this motherhood thing, but I'm getting the hang of it. To us,' Kit said. They clinked their glasses and took a long sip. Kit leaned down and picked Elijah up, holding him in her lap as she laid her head on Will's shoulder.

'Hey,' Will said, and she looked up into his face. 'What do you say we try for baby number two? I'm sure it'll be a breeze,' Will said, winking at her. She burst out laughing and then pecked him on the lips.

'We'll see,' she said. It wasn't a yes or a no. There were factors at play that meant time was of the essence, but right now, Kit was content with her little family and the life they'd built together. Will's phone pinged with a notification, quickly followed by another, then another. He glanced at his phone, and his mouth opened and closed.

'What is it? Is something wrong?' Kit asked. Will shook his head.

'Nothing's wrong. We just might need to put the baby-making on hold for a bit.'

'Why?' Kit asked. Will said nothing. Instead, he held up his phone and showed her the barrage of support in the comments of the latest video he'd posted of her singing in the pub. She looked at him, her teeth biting her bottom lip. Maybe they would have to change their plans after all.

Also by Alicia Hitchcock:

Barbed Wire and Brumbies

Not My Circus (Coming in 2026)

Sanderson Ridge Series

Orange Sky: Sanderson Ridge Prequel

The Growing Season

Lessons in Resilience (Coming in 2026)

About the Author

Armed with an overactive imagination and a concerning amount of coffee, Australian author Alicia Hitchcock creates historical and contemporary novels filled with emotionally captivating drama, high-stakes tension, and heartfelt romance.

When not travelling through time and space on the page, Alicia can be found exploring historical sites and modern cafés with equal enthusiasm, people-watching and gathering stories that blur the boundaries between then and now.

Learn more at aliciahitchcock.com and connect with her on Facebook and Instagram to keep up to date.